THE INBOX II

Daniel Ortiz

The Inbox II

First Edition Paperback ISBN: 979-8889145824-6

E-book ISBN: 979-8889145817-8

Table of Contents

Chapter 1

Waiting Game

A golden sunset lingered over the horizon, casting a warm glow on the café window. Inside, Elliot sat, his fingers tapping restlessly on the wooden table. His eyes fixed on the two latte mugs before him.

He picked one, savoring the sweet flavors that reminded him of the holiday season. The other cup remained untouched, waiting for Samara.

She should be here by now. He glanced around the room anxiously.

Elliot couldn't help but let out a sly chuckle, knowing that today was Devon's big day to ask Samara to move in together.

His only mission was to keep her distracted at the café until Devon returned from his viewing with the mysterious realtor, Belladonna.

This made Elliot wonder, *Should I tell Devon about Belladonna?* She had been flooding Elliot's inbox with messages for the last few days.

I think it's best to keep this one to myself. He began to nail-bite.

Lost in his thoughts, Elliot let out a grunt and stood up from his chair. He stepped outside, seeking solace in the open air, pacing back and forth. He pondered, "But what if I do tell him? Would it change our friendship?"

At that moment, his cell phone chimed, interrupting his anxious thoughts. It was a text message from Devon:

> Devon: I'm beginning to have second thoughts about this.

> Elliot: Relax. This is your first apartment tour. Feeling a bit anxious is totally normal. How's the neighborhood?

> Devon: Yeah, you're right. The neighborhood gives me the creeps. I ran into a really strange man on my way here. The look on his face gave me this uneasy feeling.

> Elliot: Well, you know what they say: interesting encounters make for great stories, lol.

> Devon: No offense, but I think I've had my fair share of interesting encounters. Anyway, I'm standing outside the building, but Belladonna is nowhere in sight. Maybe I should turn back.

Elliot: Belladonna's probably running a little late. Remember, this viewing could be the one that leads you to your first apartment! Just hang tight and think about how happy you and Samara will be.

Devon: OK. Please don't blow my cover.
I really want this to be a surprise. I can't wait to see Samara's reaction. I'll be back to meet you two at the café soon.

Elliot: Your secret is safe with me. By the way, is there any update on Samara? It feels like I've been waiting here forever.

Suddenly, a sweet voice called from ahead, "Elliot, is that you?"

Elliot glanced up; his eyes widened with shock. It was Samara. "Samara. You're here! I-I mean, of course, you're here," Elliot stammered, placing his phone into his pocket.

"Yeah, my mom just dropped me off. What are you doing here at the café? You don't normally come here." She gave a quizzical stare.

"Are you kidding me? I love this place." Elliot said, mopping sweat off his forehead.

"Is everything cool?" Samara interrupted. "What's got you so twitchy?"

"Twitchy? I'm not twitchy—why would I be twitchy?" Elliot blinked rapidly and cleared his throat.

"You know something, don't you?" Samara gave Elliot a playful push.

"I do not," Elliot insisted.

"Oh, come on, like Devon didn't tell you about our big fight the other day," Samara said, crossing her arms.

Elliot shook his head, jamming his hands into his pockets, "I have no clue what you're talking about, my friend." He shrugged.

Samara turned her eyes to look inside the café window. "Anyway, we're supposed to meet here." She paused. "I don't see Devon inside, and he isn't responding to my texts."

Elliot's mind raced as he desperately tried to devise a way to stall Samara. Letting out a long, shaking sigh, he leaned toward Samara. "Let's go inside and look for him," Elliot said, aware Devon wasn't inside but choosing to buy some time. He rushed to the café's entrance door, pulling it open. "Ladies first." He gestured a hand, smiling nervously.

"Thank you," Samara muttered, rolling her eyes. She wore a denim jacket, a green knit sweater, and ripped skinny jeans.

Samara strolled past Elliot, entering the café. The irresistible aroma of freshly brewed coffee filled the air. "Ahh, I just love the smell of freshly brewed coffee." Samara's eyes scanned every corner of the café, but Devon was nowhere to be seen. Samara then narrowed her eyes at Elliot. "I knew it. He's not here."

Elliot's lips quivered; a hesitant pause lingered in the air.

"I should've known coming here was a mistake." Samara lowered her head.

Elliot motioned to his table. "Come and take a seat." He pulled out a chair. "There's something you need to know before thinking of walking out of here."

Samara approached the table, her steps slow and deliberate, clearly reflecting her annoyance. She then sprawled onto the chair.

Elliot tittered nervously, "First thing—It's been a while. How are you?"

Samara's piercing stare sent a tremor through Elliot's body. *She's on to me.* His palms began to sweat.

"Hold on a minute. Did you just grab someone else's table? I don't think we ordered these drinks—and a white rose?" Samara pointed it out.

Elliot gave a short chuckle, "Well, that rose was actually left there for you by Devon. He put it there, and the lattes, too."

Samara let out a deep breath, "Enough! Will you just tell me what's going on already?" Samara urged. "Explain to me why Devon isn't here and why you're here instead," she pressed her elbows onto the table, eager to hear what he had to say.

Elliot swallowed nervously. "Absolutely, I'll explain everything, but why don't you have a drink first," Elliot said, pointing to the cups. "It's your favorite flavor—apple cinnamon." Letting out a crooked smile, Elliot slid a cup to Samara.

Samara gripped her cup and sipped her latte, watching Elliot over the rim.

There's no way I could lie to Samara. She knows me too well.

Elliot took in a deep breath and, without hesitation, blurted out. "Devon wants you to know he is deeply sorry about the other night."

Samara's eyebrow shot up, "So, you do know about our big fight?"

Elliot hesitated, "All right, you got me. But I've only got bits and pieces to the story."

Samara stood watching. "So, what else do you know?"

Elliot's eyes wandered as he mustered the courage to spill the words. "I just can't keep this inside any longer!" he exclaimed, his voice filled with remorse.

Samara's eyes widened with confusion as she stared at Elliot. "What on earth are you talking about?"

Elliot leaned back, his chest expanding as he took a deep breath and slowly released it. "Look. Devon didn't want you to know this, but. . .he is planning to move out from his dorm and into an apartment of his own."

Samara's eyes grew with surprise. "What? Why wouldn't he tell me this? I—"

Elliot swiftly interrupted, cutting her off mid-sentence. "Hold on! Before you say anything, there is more." Elliot chuckled nervously. "He's also hoping you'll move in with him, too. Right now. Well, not right now, but when he finds a place. So, it would help if you sat tight here until he's done with his first viewing." Elliot's hands swept through the air as he exclaimed, "That's it!"

Samara shrieked in delight, "So, he's at his first viewing right now? I can't believe it!" her voice echoed through the small café walls.

"Well, you wanted the truth—Devon will be back here to break the news to you himself. I'm just waiting on his cue."

Samara sneered with delight. "This explains why he's been so out of it the last few days. The secret phone calls and anxious behavior. It was right before me the entire time."

Elliot understood that telling Samara would have severe consequences but felt trapped with no other options. He glanced at the entrance of the café.

"Wouldn't it be funny if Devon walked in right now?" He let out a forced, fake laugh.

Samara sprung up from her chair. She lifted the white rose from the table, held it up her nose, and sniffed. "I need to apologize for the harsh things I said to him the other night. Ugh, God, I was so stupid." She carefully tucked the white rose inside her jacket pocket.

Elliot responded, "I recall Devon mentioning something about an offensive message posted under his account. Was that what started the fight?"

Samara paused and sat down in her chair again. "Yes. . . and I know you heard about my dramatic reaction."

"Remember, I only got a glimpse of the story," Elliot said.

"I should probably call him and apologize again. I know he wouldn't do anything to hurt me." Samara grabbed her phone from her pocket before Elliot intervened.

"Hold that dial, señorita!" he shouted, leaping from his chair to grab her phone.

Samara raised her hands and leaned back, "Easy there, big guy."

Elliot slumped into his chair. "You cannot call him. Devon can't know about anything we talked about. So, you'll just have to act surprised when he breaks the news. He'd kill me if he found out I told you!" he took a deep breath.

Samara crossed her arms, "OK, fine. I won't say anything."

Elliot muttered to himself, feeling regretful.

Who am I kidding? Samara is a leaky faucet. She won't be able to keep this to herself.

He reached into his pocket for his phone, hoping for an update from Devon, when he saw there was a message. "Oh no!" Elliot said sternly.

At that moment, Samara rose, fed up. "On second thought, scratch that. I can't do this whole 'waiting game,'" she air quoted. "If Devon wants to chat, he can come over to my place and talk."

Elliot jumped to his feet and tugged on Samara's sleeve. "Don't go." He tried to explain but could only raise his phone for Samara to read Devon's urgent message:

Get me out of here!

Elliot sucked in his breath. "He may be in trouble. We should check on him."

Samara scoffed, "So, now you're giving me permission to join you?" She said with a sarcastic tone.

Elliot paused to rub his hands over his face.

"Yes. Devon could be in actual danger for all we know."

Samara darted her way toward the exit door. "Well, in that case, I'm already ten steps ahead of you."

"Tsk. Wait up for me." Elliot jogged from behind.

Chapter 2

Shadow man

A gray and eerie twilight sky hovered over the neighborhood. The air had a crisp bite to it.

"Late autumn nights are always so cold," Samara crossed her arms, hunching her shoulders from the chill. "Hopefully, Devon's not too far." She shivered involuntarily.

Elliot found solace in a shadowy corner, monitoring Devon's location. "He did share his location with me. Hang on, I'll tell you where we're going in just a second."

Samara took a curious look around the street. An old streetlight flickered from across the way. She turned around to see Elliot staring at his cell phone screen. "What does the GPS say?" Samara asked.

"My GPS tells me the place is right down that street." Elliot pointed toward the flickering streetlight. The path before them was gloomy and unwelcoming.

Samara's voice quaked. "That's very dark. Can't you just drive us there in your truck?" Elliot's voice dropped to a whisper, "We can, but oddly enough, I'm pretty sure that's the same street where I parked it."

Samara took in a sharp breath, "So, we'll need to head in that direction regardless. I guess we don't need the GPS after all, right?" she shoved her freezing hands into her pockets. Elliot's face twisted in confusion.

"Why do you seem so confused?" Samara asked.

Elliot stood paused beneath the streetlight. "I'm not so sure. The street looks a lot different at night."

Samara's breath hung in the frigid air, "Well then, let's follow the GPS. I'm sure it'll take us directly to Devon and your truck," She took a step forward while Elliot followed through with the GPS that led them deeper into the darkness.

Samara reached for her phone in her pocket and switched on the LED flash feature. "It's not enough light, but at least we can watch our steps." The flashlight barely illuminated their path.

Elliot's eyes followed the navigator on his phone.

"So, how long have you known?" Samara asked, shining her light directly on Elliot's face.

He shielded his eyes from the light with one hand. "Ugh, know about what? And could you please turn the flash away from me?"

Samara grinned. "You know. Devon, finding us an apartment." She elbowed him.

Elliot shook his head, his eyes filled with regret, "I can't. I've already said too much."

"Boo. You suck!" Samara said, shifting her flashlight ahead. "Well, I guess you have said much more than you were supposed to."

There was blackness all around; the glow from the flashlight seemed to fade away the deeper they wandered into the darkness.

"Dammit! The GPS is recalculating," he shouted.

Samara handed her phone over to Elliot. "We can always use my phone if yours troubles you. Just insert the address."

Elliot typed in the location on Samara's phone when, at that moment, he heard footsteps approaching. "What was that?"

Samara slicked on a lip balm she pulled from her jacket. "What was what?"

"It sounded like footsteps." Elliot froze.

Samara grabbed her phone from Elliot. "I sure hope they were footsteps. Maybe we can ask for directions instead of relying on a stubborn GPS."

Suddenly, Samara also heard footsteps echoing through the dark street. Startled, she turned to see where the sound had come from.

Elliot's voice dropped to a whisper, "Tell me you heard that now?"

The sound of dead leaves crunching underfoot had stopped.

"I did. Maybe it's a street cat or something?" Samara said, her eyes fixed on Elliot.

"Um, that was no cat," Elliot's voice quivered. "On second thought, I'm beginning to think this isn't the same street where I parked my truck." He said in a hushed tone.

Elliot quickly turned on the flashlight feature on his phone, but there was no sight of anyone around. He could hear Samara's shaking breath. Suddenly, footsteps grew louder and closer before a lopsided shadow appeared just a few steps behind them.

Elliot spun quickly to face the man without hesitation.

"Elliot, wait!" Samara cried out. Elliot paused. The shadowed figure stood in utter silence.

Samara sucked in the cold air and let it out slowly. "Sir, can you help us, please? I think we're lost. We're looking for 323 Roebling Street. Can you point us in the right direction?" Samara said impatiently.

Elliot waved his flashlight above his head.

Suddenly, the stranger stepped into the glow of the phone's light. He wore a hood garment, which made it difficult to discern his features. Samara and Elliot lost their footing and stumbled backward.

"Poor souls." He said, his tone was soft but lethal. His gaze sent chills down Samara's spine. Samara gasped, grabbing Elliot's hand to steady herself.

"We don't want any trouble. Can-can you please tell us which way to go?" Samara stammered.

A frosty haze escaped the stranger's mouth, swirling in the chilly air around him. His hood curtained his eyes; while raising a smirk, he pointed forward. "Straight ahead," he said in a croaky voice.

"All right, well. . . thanks." There was a slight hesitation in Elliot's voice as he hooked Samara's arm, and they hurried away.

"What a creep. Is he following us?" Samara asked.

Elliot turned his eyes back.

"No way! That's freakin' unbelievable!" Elliot looked startled for a moment and then composed himself.

"What is it?" Samara's voice quivered.

"I don't know how, but he vanished," Elliot paused as his eyes scanned the dark, empty street.

"Good! Now let's speed up the pace," Samara demanded. "I'm starting to get a sense that this neighborhood might not be the safest," Her footsteps echoed through the empty street, urgency in every stride.

"Something about that man didn't seem right, don't you think?" Elliot looked back over his shoulder one last time.

"Well, duh, something was totally off about him," Samara agreed.

Suddenly, she came to a stop near a welcome streetlight. The wind gusted through the tree above, sending a shower of withered leaves down upon her.

"I think that's the house. Right there . . . across the street," Samara said, brushing away the fallen leaves. The address number reflected in the dim streetlight, 323.

Elliot nodded. "That is the place."

"Seems . . . ordinary," Samara added. She stared wide-eyed at the house as they strolled toward it.

"Yeah, nothing like the other dilapidated houses lined up on this street," Elliot said perplexedly. "This street seems familiar to me now," He paused and rubbed his eyes with his hands. "My truck is definitely parked somewhere around here."

"Well, good. At least we can drive back. I never want to cross paths with that creep guy again." Samara said as she approached the front steps of the building.

Elliot reached out and grasped her arm, softly pulling her back.

"I'm not too sure if we're allowed in."

Samara's confusion was evident as she looked at Elliot and exclaimed, "What the heck are you talking about?"

Elliot replied, "Devon said something about a 'no visitors' policy—something like that."

Samara scoffed. "Oh, come on! Do you seriously think I came all this way just to not go inside? You can't be for real right now," Samara laughed. "I'm going inside, rules or no rules." She plodded her way up the stairs.

"Wait!" Elliot pointed toward the doorway as he rushed to her side. "Look! The doorknob. . .it's rattling!"

Samara turned her eyes toward the door, and when it swung open, she gasped and clutched Elliot's hand.

"What the hell are you doing here!" Devon exclaimed, pushing Elliot back.

Samara and Elliot burst into laughter.

"Ha-ha! Devon, you almost gave us a heart attack!" Elliot caught his breath, "I got your 'get me out of here' text and it freaked me out. I thought you might be in danger! We just had to make sure you were safe," he explained.

Devon stepped out of the building and slammed the door shut behind him.

"Babe, I couldn't wait to see you!" Samara draped her arms around Devon's neck and kissed his cheek. "Elliot told me what you've been up to."

Devon rolled his eyes. "What are you talking about?"

Looking down, Elliot pretended not to listen.

Devon glared at Elliot. "You told her?"

"I had to—she was interrogating me with all these questions. I don't do well with questions—you know that. As you can see, it worked, too." Elliot pointed at Samara with her arms wrapped around Devon.

"Is everything okay? You ran out of there like you'd seen a ghost or something." Elliot asked.

"Everything's fine. I just wouldn't recommend this place to anybody," Devon said sharply.

"Well, what are the odds? There goes my truck!" Elliot shouted, noticing it parked down the street. Elliot bolted towards it, "All right, love birds. Let's get out of here. Something about this neighborhood gives me the heebie-jeebies," he said, hopping inside his truck.

The three entered Elliot's truck as Samara cuddled with Devon in the back seat.

"Bro, you're not going to believe it, but I think we actually came face-to-face with that creepy guy you mentioned over text," Elliot chuckled.

"That encounter was seriously unsettling, to say the least," Samara added, letting out a nervous laugh.

Devon sat quietly, as if he had zoned out of the conversation.

Elliot was ready to drive off when his phone sent an alarming notification. He looked at it and turned to Devon and Samara. With a rush of excitement, he gathered their attention, "Listen up, guys! I have something important I want to share." his voice filled with anticipation,

Devon and Samara leaned forward to listen.

Elliot proceeded, "After hearing about your plans to move in together, I think I'm ready to do the same."

Samara cut in, "You can't room us," she said sarcastically.

"I know. That totally came out the wrong way," Elliot snickered, "What I meant to say is that I'm ready to kick off my own apartment search," Elliot said, his voice rising in excitement.

"So, what's your game plan for finding an apartment?" Devon asked—his eyes locked with Elliot in the rearview mirror.

"A local realtor. She's kind of already reached out and offered me a place. . .I think."

"Wow, that was quick," Samara said.

"Well, where exactly is this place?" Devon questioned.

Elliot chuckled, "It's funny you even ask because I don't have the slightest clue. What I do know is that it's in the area. I actually have some photos that were sent to me. Want to check them out?"

Devon's voice took a severe tone, "No, I don't. What is the name of the person you're supposed to meet, the realtor?" Devon insisted.

Samara could see Devon's hands begin to tremble. "Babe, is something wrong?" She leaned forward, gently placing a hand on Devon's shoulder.

Elliot ignored Devon's question.

I've got to pretend I don't know anything from here on out. I cannot mention Belladonna. Devon will totally freak out.

Elliot started the engine and began to drive off. "She's just a local realtor. We've been communicating back and forth through e-mail."

"Open your damn inbox and show me the messages!" Devon demanded.

Elliot's pulse quickened, "I am driving—give me a second." Elliot's eyes went back and forth from the road ahead to his phone. He knew he had let his big mouth get the best of him again.

At that moment, Devon snatched Elliot's phone from his hand and read the message out loud on the screen.

Hello Elliot,
Are you available to meet tomorrow? Does 5:30
p.m. fit into your schedule?
    - Belladonna

"5:30? Hmm, I'm not sure if that time works. I'll have to reschedule," Elliot let out a shaky laugh.

Devon pulled himself forward, grabbing tight to Elliot's shoulder. "I can't believe you went ahead and did this!"

"What are you talking about?" Elliot laughed nervously. His eyes darted to Devon in the rearview mirror.

"Babe, what's going on?" Samara asked, watching Devon's face, masked in shock.

"It's a trap!" The air around Devon suddenly seemed hard to breathe. "You-you can't meet with her," Devon stammered.

"Bro, you seem nervous. And what do you mean by 'it's a trap'?" Elliot asked, his expression quizzical.

Devon panted, his words coming out in rapid bursts. "The realtor, Belladonna!" Devon shouted. "It's one huge scam. . . don't fall for it."

Elliot replied, "Wait, hold up! Are you telling me that all those e-mails and phone calls with that realtor, Belladonna, turned out to be a scam?" Elliot shook his head.

Fear fluttered through Devon, and his gaze flew to Samara.

"Devon, you're not looking so great. We have to find a place to pull over right now!" Samara demanded, watching Devon with concern.

Things around Devon seemed to fade as he grew dizzy and nauseous. He could hear his breathing growing heavier, louder, and stronger.

Elliot stopped the truck immediately in the middle of the road. He glanced back at Devon, worried, when suddenly a thunderous crash echoed, and heavy raindrops began to pour down. Devon's vision blurred; he could no longer recognize the faces around him as the noises and voices grew muffled. His eyes rolled back, and darkness engulfed him.

Chapter 3

Devon's Nightmare

Devon's eyelids fluttered open as he slowly regained consciousness. He felt disoriented, his mind struggling to make sense of his surroundings as he huddled on the ground, surrounded by a musty cellar-like smell. He slowly picked himself up.

"Where am I?" his shaken voice echoed through the darkness as he realized the nightmare was not over. He found himself transported back to the exact location where he had met Belladonna.

"But I got away! This cannot be happening again!"

Terrified, Devon screamed, "Samara, Elliot!" but there was no response. He covered his face with his hands and sobbed, despair sounding through the empty pitch-black room. Throwing his hands up, he shouted once more, "What do you want from me!"

There was a long silence before a bone-curdling laugh bounced off the dark walls.

Devon turned quickly. At that moment, footsteps thundered on the cold ground, growing closer toward him when suddenly they stopped.

His chest was heaving, and his mouth felt dry as cotton. Frightened, Devon took a deep breath and closed his eyes. With clenched fists, he cried out at the top of his lungs.

"Help! Let me out!"

Suddenly, he felt a chilling grip as cold, demon hands forcefully pinned him to the ground, trapping his legs and feet. It was Belladonna.

The succubus then snarled into his ear.

"Get off of me!" Devon shouted. The look of her gray face—her jagged smile and dark, empty eyes—sent shivers throughout Devon's body. He grappled with the hands that pressed down on him.

Then he remembered the onyx ring.

It can banish her again. He thought.

"If only I could reach for my pocket!"

Unable to shake off the force that gripped his body, he finally broke a hand free and swung a fist into the air. He felt it strike but wasn't sure if it was Belladonna. With eyes tightly shut, he took another swing, certain he'd strike the succubus.

"Let me go!" Devon screamed, flinging his hands around in a fury.

"I'm not letting you go!" The voice declared.

"Open your eyes and look at me!" The voice went from evil to sweet.

Devon refrained from struggling.

"Samara. Is that you?" Devon said, catching his breath. He couldn't make out his surroundings through his blurred vision but soon realized he was safe again.

"Where am I?" Devon asked, opening his eyes wide.

The sound of raindrops bounced off the truck's windshield.

"We're still inside the truck," Samara replied.

Devon saw a puzzled Samara and Elliot staring down at him.

"Bro, you went into a huge blowout just now. You even knocked me in the jaw a couple of times, too. Ow!" Elliot said, rubbing the side of his face, "We had to hold you down—it was wild. Should we take you to a hospital or something?"

"Hospital? Are you kidding? I-I'm fine," Devon stuttered. "Could you guys just . . . you know. Let me go now?" Devon directed his eyes toward his left arm, where Elliot had been holding him down. Samara's body pressed against Devon's torso with all her strength, holding him tightly in her grip.

"I'll back off; just don't throw any more punches," Elliot replied, his voice tinged with a hint of warning.

The two helped Devon sit against the back seat.

"It was terrifying. Your screams and awful cries, I never heard anything like it before. Are you sure you're all right?" Devon could see the worry in Samara's eyes.

"I'm OK. I just need to get some rest, that's all."

Samara and Elliot turned and eyed one another. "Is that all you'll say about what just happened?" Elliot asked.

Devon nodded, "Yes. What else do you expect me to say?"

Elliot exited from the back seat and returned to the driver's seat.

"Can I ask you something?" Samara turned her eyes to Devon.

"What's up?"

"You want to tell us what really happened to you in that apartment?"

"What do you mean?" Devon exhaled deeply.

"You know what I mean. You've been shaking like a leaf since running out of there." Devon made a loud sigh and crossed his arms. He shut his eyes and laid his head on Samara's lap.

"Are you seriously brushing me off?" Samara said in disbelief.

The only thing Devon could think of was to lie—make up a story and hope that both Elliot and Samara would somehow forget.

"Nothing happened in that apartment," Devon drew a deep breath. "So please, just drop it."

Samara shook her head, "You're unbelievable."

Elliot turned his eyes to Samara through his rearview mirror. "Samara's right. You did run out of there in a panic," Elliot added.

"I don't know what you guys are talking about," Devon said, rubbing his eyes with both hands.

"I was in no panic. Ugh, just take me to my car, please. I'm parked right next to the café."

Elliot nodded in agreement while adjusting the rearview mirror. "Fine!" he said sternly. There was a short silence when suddenly the truck engine spluttered, and tires squealed down the road.

"Elliot, what the hell is wrong with you? Are you crazy!" Samara shouted.

Elliot barreled down the slippery, wet road. "We're heading back. I'd put on your seatbelt if I were you." Elliot's eyes fixed heavily on the road. It was almost as if he had gone into a trance.

"This isn't funny!" Devon leaned forward and firmly gripped Elliot's shoulder.

"Don't do that," Elliot spoke gruffly.

"Elliot, slow down. You're going to crash us. Devon, make him stop, please!" Samara begged; her eyes widened in fear.

Elliot gave the truck more gas, darting alongside another vehicle.

"OK, I'll tell you what happened if you stop now!" Devon exclaimed.

Elliot rounded a curve, slamming the brakes. The truck jerked violently forward, the impact sending Samara and Devon out from their seats and onto the floorboard.

"Have you lost your goddamned mind?" Samara cried, lifting her body onto the seat with one hand. "You almost got us killed!"

Elliot responded with a hint of sarcasm. "Almost, but it didn't happen," Elliot replied.

Rain splattered against the truck, drawing Devon's attention outside. He tried to peer through the window, but it was too blurry.

"Where are we?" Samara rolled down the car window. "Ugh, why are we back at the creepy neighborhood?" Samara raised an eyebrow.

"There's something Devon isn't telling us about that apartment," Elliot said sternly.

"Oh, come on, Elliot, you heard him. The place was a scam. Let's just forget it now," Samara said, rolling up the window.

"Did you not see what happened to your boyfriend tonight? Didn't that worry you?" Elliot turned his head over his shoulder and looked sternly at Samara. "Everything is not okay. I know it, and you know it, so either Devon tells us what's really happening, or I can go inside and find out for myself."

Elliot opened the truck's door, removing the keys from the ignition.

"You can't go in there!" Devon shouted.

Elliot turned his eyes to Devon and paused.

"Watch me."

Chapter 4

Don't go in there!

"Please don't go inside!" Devon yelled, rolling down the car window.

"Give me one good reason why I shouldn't?" Elliot said, crossing his arms.

"Because, the place, it's -it's infested." Devon stammered.

Elliot's eyes bulged, "What? What do you mean it's infested?"

Devon's words spilled out in a single breath, "There's maggots, flies, cockroaches, and spiders. It's gross, and there's a stench. Incredibly nauseating. That's why I came out of there the way I did. Things were falling from the ceiling and crawling all over me. It's a complete nightmare. Trust me; you don't want to go in there," his voice rushed urgently.

Elliot's eyes widened in disbelief. "How is that even possible?"

Devon quickly interjected, "Oh, it's possible," he nodded dramatically. "There were snakes and rats everywhere, huddled together in a corner, too. They were all feasting on each other or something else—who knows? Anyway, the place is a complete rip-off!" Devon expressed his narrative using his hands. "It's embarrassing. I don't want to say anything more about it before Samara." Devon stared into Samara's eyes. His nostrils flared. He kept his head down, letting out a soft sniff, pretending to be hurt. "It's not the surprise I wanted to give," his voice lowered, "There's really nothing to see in there. So, we should just leave?"

Elliot pointed a finger at Devon, "You had me at the snake part."

"I hate snakes!" Elliot exclaimed.

Elliot threw his hands up in mock defeat, "All right. You win. I guess there's really nothing to see after all," Elliot hopped back into the driver's seat.

"Oh, believe me, you're not missing a single thing," Devon echoed.

A prolonged silence followed their drive back.

Devon stared out the window, pensive. He let out a long sigh of despair.

I know Elliot isn't buying my cover story. I could almost hear his thoughts about the whole thing. He never did take me seriously. He never believed anything I had to say about Belladonna. Otherwise, why would he be messaging her?

The thought of Belladonna immediately made Devon's stomach churn with unease. Belladonna was out for blood, and she wasn't going to stop. A stab of sheer terror came over

Devon. He stretched out a hand to Samara and squeezed it tightly. "You know, I'd never let anything bad happen to you, right?" He said, gazing at her intently.

Samara grinned. "I know that," she whispered.

Devon pulled in closer and draped an arm around her shoulders. "Spend the night with me?" Devon insisted.

Samara looked into Devon's eyes, pausing for a moment.

"Is something wrong?" Devon asked.

"I'm beginning to worry about you," she replied.

Devon swallowed a lump in his throat and turned his eyes away from Samara. Before he could reply, Elliot interrupted, pulling his truck into the café parking lot, "Did you say you parked around here? I hope we find your car."

"Yes. You can drop me off here. It's fine," Devon nodded.

Elliot's gaze shifted towards Samara, "Are you crashing at Devon's tonight, or do you need a lift back home?" Elliot asked.

"I think you already know the answer to that question," Samara chuckled, stepping out of the truck.

Devon lingered for a few seconds. "Look, I just want to say that I'm sorry. . . you know, for causing a scene back there," he said, with his head lowered.

"It's all good. We all have our moments." Elliot replied, feeling a bit remorseful.

"Of course," Devon laughed nervously, "Just please promise me you won't go back to that apartment or answer any of Belladonna's e-mails right now. I need your word."

Elliot's eyes locked onto Devon's worried expression. "You have my word. You've got to be nuts if you think I'm going anywhere near a place infested with snakes. There's no way!" Elliot assured.

Devon stepped away from Elliot and caught up with Samara.

Elliot's eyes turned to the truck's side view mirror as he watched Samara and Devon stroll away. Thunder rumbled as he sat parked outside the café, pensive.

But what if the snake story was merely a fabricated lie? he thought.

Rain continued to pattern on the truck's windshield.

I've known Devon my whole life, and never have I seen him this shaken up. It couldn't just be Belladonna causing this. There had to be something more.

The engine sound from his old RAM truck roared, echoing throughout the quiet streets.

Elliot winced and rubbed his forehead, letting out a short grunt. Suddenly, his eyes caught something whirl to the side of his truck. Sensing something eerie, Elliot sat upright and turned his eyes to the side-view mirrors, but no one was there.

He opened the car door halfway and shouted, "Hello?" Elliot waited for a response.

"I could've sworn I saw something there."

Uncertain and suspicious, he stepped out of his truck as the engine ran and took one last look around the lot.

There was nothing in sight.

"It was probably my imagination." He thought.

He hopped back into his truck, switched the radio, and drove off.

Chapter 5

A Visit from Death

The rain picked up, drumming wildly on the truck's rooftop. The windshield wipers swished back and forth. Suddenly, one wiper jammed midway through, sweeping away the rain.

"Damn wipers!" Elliot sucked in a deep breath; luckily, he wasn't too far from home.

At that moment, an old familiar song came on the radio.

Elliot cranked up the volume even more, belting the lyrics with gusto. "Man, they just don't make music like this anymore!" he shouted.

Suddenly, a crackle on the radio interrupted his tune. "Goddamn radio." He let out a grunt. His gaze traveled to the rearview mirror, where a dark figure sat still in the quiet. The shadowed figure gave a monstrous grin, revealing narrow, sharp teeth as it glowered at Elliot. Terrified with shock, Elliot turned his eyes back to the road. He tried to utter a word, but then . . . it spoke.

"Never miss a ring when she calls, for the flesh you wear, she'll rip down to your bones,"

The croaky tone sent chills down Elliot's spine. His body grew cold and numb, losing sensation in his hands. The truck hurtled its way through the heavy rainstorm.

"Who are you?" Elliot shouted. He pressed his foot down on the brakes, but the truck throttled full speed.

"No!" Elliot cried out.

The moment seemed to go at a lumbering pace, but his thoughts were racing.

"Is this how I'm going to die?" His ninth birthday tore into his panicked mind. Maybe because it was the last year he would see his mom alive, Elliot felt his throat tighten at the memory of her—her touch, her smell, and her beautiful, bright smile.

I miss her so much.

Tears began to fill his eyes.

Dad hadn't been the same since she'd been gone. None of us were the same after her fatal car accident; now it's happening again.

Elliot held onto the steering wheel, gripping it with all his might.

He felt his heart racing uncontrollably as he glanced at the mirror, only to find the shadowy figure disappear into a cloud of dark smoke. It was like a visit from death itself, with a cryptic message that haunted Elliot, filling every fiber of his being with bone chilling fear.

Chapter 6

Evil Falls

Elliot kept his foot pressed on the brakes, and the truck abruptly halted, slinging his body forward, his head striking the side window.

"Ouch!" He moaned, feeling a warm trickle of blood running down his brow. He pressed a hand on the wound, feeling a sharp stabbing pain.

"What was that thing?"

The truck's engine suddenly went out. Elliot struggled with the door handle before exiting the truck, sliding his legs out one by one. The rain continued to pour heavily. He searched around aimlessly, dizzy. With a swift motion, he swung open the rear side door, poking his head inside quickly. There was no one there. He returned to the driver's side and slumped into his seat.

"Now what?" Elliot blew out air in frustration and then looked around.

Suddenly, bright headlights flashed in the mirror, approaching from behind as he blotted at his wound. A small car passed steadily alongside Elliot's truck, halted in the middle of the long, empty road. The passenger rolled down their car window midway.

"Are you all right, boy?" A scratchy voice called out from the shadowed driver's seat.

Elliot groaned, lowering down a window for a better look, but could only see the stranger's wrinkly hands lit up from the shimmering moonlight.

"I'm all right. Thank you for asking, ma'am," he said with a grunt as he dropped his head back against the headrest.

"Do you need me to call your father?"

Elliot peered cautiously at the car for a few seconds. He then recognized the 1970 yellow Pinto. "Ms. James, is that you?"

Ms. James leaned into the moon's glow, revealing herself. "Yes. It is me." She stared intensely. "Aren't you Aaron's boy?" She pointed, squinting her eyes.

"I am." Elliot's expression indicated pain, but he gave a wry smile.

"Are you injured?" Ms. James hunched over her steering wheel, staring at Elliot, awaiting a response.

The rain suddenly stopped, and a piercing silence followed. A light wind whispered across the trees, and a dark cloud drifted over the moon's light, turning the road into complete blackness.

"Oh my," Ms. James said coldly. "Great evil has descended upon us." Her face was paralyzed with fear.

"What do you mean?" Elliot asked, his face filled with confusion.

Ms. James locked eyes with Elliot. "She arrives stealthily, like a nocturnal thief, to snatch up souls." Ms. James explained, her voice dry and cold.

Elliot stared up at the dark cloud that hovered over them. A chill ran down his spine, and his heart began to race. He could feel an eerie presence surrounding him.

"You've seen her, haven't you?" Terror washed over Ms. James' face.

"No-no," Elliot stammered. "Ugh, Ms. James, thanks for your concern, but I think I better go," Elliot rolled up his window, but before he could close it shut, a loud growl rose from a distance, unlike anything Elliot had heard before.

"What was that thing?" He turned quickly to Ms. James, who remained silently parked alongside his truck.

Ms. James recoiled, her eyes petrified. "It's her. . ."

"Who?" Elliot asked as he struggled to start the engine.

"Young man, that thing you just heard won't stop until it gets what it wants," Ms. James glowered at Elliot.

"Well, what is it?" Elliot's curiosity was piqued as his engine roared back to life.

"A creature from the abyss, more horrifying than any mortal has ever witnessed." Ms. James's trembling hands clutched the steering wheel tightly.

Elliot's heart pounded as he listened to Ms. James's chilling warning, his mind filled with unease. Still unable to shake off the unsettling image of the dark figure he saw in the rearview mirror.

"She emerges under the cloak of darkness and preys upon unsuspecting souls like yours. Beware of the succubus!" she said with a raspy tone.

"Succubus!" Elliot's voice cracked as he exclaimed, "You cannot be serious right now."

Ms. James scolded, "Open your eyes, boy! This town has been haunted for years by this demon, and . . ." she paused dramatically, pointing a trembling finger at Elliot, "And you're next!"

Lighting suddenly flashed around them.

Ms. James continued, "She craves the body and soul of young men like you."

Elliot's mind raced, thinking, "What in the world is she even talking about?"

Ms. James' voice filled with regret as she continued, "Oh dear, this is all my fault. I couldn't—I just didn't have enough courage to do it."

Without warning, she maneuvered her car around Elliot's truck and sped down the road.

For a moment, Elliot stood paused. "OK, I think I've had enough for one night." Elliot chuckled in disbelief, ready to leave the eerie atmosphere behind. He pulled off the brakes and drove home.

Chapter 7

The Warning

Later that night, Elliot parked his truck at his home garage, "What a crazy night," he said out loud.

At that moment, his cell phone rang—the number unknown. Elliot hesitated to answer, then he responded, "Hello?"

There was no response, only static and heavy breathing on the other end.

"Who's there?" he demanded.

A demonic snarl startled Elliot before a clear voice came in, "Can you hear me now?" It was his dad.

Elliot gave a deep sigh. "Yes, Dad, I can hear you now. What's up?" The inescapable chatter in the background drowned out his father's voice.

He pressed his ear closer to the phone. "Dad. Could you step away from the noise? It's hard to hear you with all that commotion."

"Oh, sorry. How about now? Is it any better?" his dad shouted.

Elliot snickered. "Yes, much better!"

"Good. I just wanted you to know that I'm working some extra hours tonight and won't be home until tomorrow morning. Put out the trash for me, would you? The waste truck comes in a little after dawn."

"You got it, pops."

"All right, Son. I'll See you tomorrow." The call ended.

Elliot stepped out of his truck and walked to the front porch. He fiddled in his pockets, searching for his house key when his cell phone rang again.

He hadn't recognized the number but thought it could be his dad again.

"Seems like he might have missed mentioning something else," Elliot said out loud.

After the third ring, Elliot answered. "Anything else, Dad?"

He transferred the phone to his shoulder to free up his hand while unlocking the front door. He paused and waited, but there was still no reply. Elliot entered the house and shut the door. He then pulled the phone away from his ear to see if he was still connected to the call. He was.

"OK, I guess this is a prank call then," Elliot said sternly. "I know you're there. I can hear you breathing," he said, returning the phone to his ear.

The line went quiet, but before Elliot could hang up, a distorted, gravelly voice came through the phone: "I am watching. . ."

Elliot turned his body, glancing in all directions as the floorboards creaked.

The voice came through again. This time, it was clear. "I said, can you hear me?' It was a woman, her tone welcoming and warm.

"Yes, I can hear you." He raised his eyebrows, letting out a jet of air between flared nostrils.

"I don't think you heard me clear earlier." The woman giggled.

"I'm sorry about that. My phone has been going through some technical issues," Elliot said as he walked and talked.

"Well, I'm so happy I got a hold of you now. I've been trying to reach you."

"Have you?" Elliot scoffed.

I don't think I even got her name, Elliot thought.

"I was afraid I'd spammed your inbox with messages. How foolish of me."

Elliot chuckled. He realized he'd forgotten to lock the front door. "No, you're fine," he assured her, quickly returning to the entrance door.

Just as he reached out to twist the lock shut, the woman's voice yelled out,

"I'd like to present you with an amazing offer!" her high, enthusiastic tone alarmed and captured his undivided attention. He unconsciously turned his back to the door as it remained unlocked.

"It's Belladonna, your realtor. I hope you didn't forget about me," she chuckled.

"Oh. Right! How could I forget about you?" He laughed nervously.

Belladonna continued, "Here's the deal, Elliot, I need to fill this remarkable apartment pronto. No extra fees and no down payment. It's all yours . . . whenever you are ready."

Elliot contemplated for a moment,

Belladonna's already doing such a great job making the apartment sound fantastic. I'd be stupid if I passed on this deal.

"Elliot, are you still there?" Her voice was upbeat and cheerful.

"I'm still here," Elliot lifted his gaze and ran his fingers through his hair. "I apologize for the delay. I've been meaning to reply to your e-mail earlier today. I just needed a moment to collect my thoughts before deciding," he laughed.

Belladonna listened carefully and responded empathetically, "Life can be a whirlwind sometimes, I understand."

Ugh, who am I kidding? I should just go for it. Elliot thought.

Determined to keep it a secret from Devon, Elliot made up his mind and decided to take the offer.

"All right. I've made up my mind," Elliot said assertively, "By the way, in your last e-mail, you mentioned something about meeting tomorrow at 5:30 p.m. Unfortunately, that won't work. Is there a way we can reschedule for another day?" Elliot's voice faltered, his words filled with hesitation.

"Of course, we can reschedule," Belladonna replied.

"OK, great. In the meantime, I'll keep in touch. Thank you for calling, but I—"

Belladonna cut off Elliot's words, "But let's make it soon! I'd hate for you to miss such a wonderful deal."

Elliot began to make his way to his bedroom, situated on the lower level of the house. Suddenly, Elliot found himself completely spellbound, almost in a trance. There was just something about the realtor's voice that lured him in. She seemed even more intriguing yet obscure.

"I don't need to think twice about it. I'm definitely in!" Elliot said his decision was firm.

"Great! I'll keep your name on my list now that I have your word. Be sure to keep an eye on your inbox for more information. . .I cannot wait to have you." Belladonna hung up the phone.

Elliot's trance was instantly broken, as if someone had snapped their fingers. He paused after the call ended. "Did she say just say she cannot wait to have me? He stared at the phone, perplexed.

Once Elliot went downstairs and entered his room, it dawned on him that he had completely forgotten to do something important before the phone call interrupted. His mind went blank, leaving him unable to remember what it was.

He shrugged, "I'm pretty sure it was nothing to worry about."

Chapter 8

You're Next!

———————————

That night, Elliot slipped on some comfy sleep shorts, yawned, and switched off the lights. He left the television playing softly in the background, the dark room bathed in a soothing midnight-blue glow from the screen's light. Elliot sprawled out on his bed and drifted asleep when a husky, diabolical voice shouted, "You're next!"

A startled Elliot shouted back, "Who said that!" He scanned the room and realized it was just a television ad playing in the background. Rubbing his eye sockets with both hands, he chuckled.

He scavenged for the remote control, breathing heavily.

"Where is it?" He soon found it sitting alongside his cell phone on the edge of his nightstand and switched off the television. He checked his watch for the time; it was a quarter past midnight. Suddenly, the house phone rang from upstairs.

"Who could possibly be calling at this time?"

Elliot crawled out of bed and headed up the stairs. His tired eyes almost missed a step. He strode into the kitchen, where a light glare lit the room softly.

"Hello?" his voice cracked. He waited a few seconds. There was no reply. "Hello, is anyone there?" Elliot said for a second time. He could hear soft breathing on the other end, followed by a crackling noise. "Prank callers, again?" Elliot groaned and hung up the phone.

The phone rang again immediately. He gripped the phone and pulled it up to his ear.

"Why don't you go bother somebody else!" He shouted out.

"Elliot, is that you?" A faint voice came through.

"Who is this?" he demanded.

"Oh, thank goodness. It's Ms. James."

Confused, he asked, "Ms. James? How did you get this number?"

"Oh, dear," she chuckled softly. "Your father has had this number since you were a little boy. Back then, we used to have all the phone numbers memorized. But, nowadays, it seems your generation doesn't bother doing that anymore." She grunted.

Elliot sighed, "Ms. James. I'd love to chat, but I've got to be up early. I open for the auto shop, and I can't be late again—"

"I won't take up much of your time, dear. I just have a very important message for you.

"Okay, what's the message?" he asked.

Ms. James swallowed hard, her nerves evident, before continuing, "First, may I ask if you've spoken to the Owens boy?"

"You mean Devon?" Elliot replied.

"Yes. Have you spoken to him?" Ms. James lowered her tone.

"Wait—is there something wrong? Is Devon okay?" Elliot's face clouded with concern.

Ms. James took a deep breath and whispered, "That young man knows."

"What does he know?" Elliot peeked from the kitchen to the dark hallway. He could see the moonlight shine through the front door glaze.

"Belladonna," Ms. James said in a raspy voice.

Ms. James paused. "That name still haunts me to this day."

There is no way Ms. James' referring to Belladonna, the realtor. That'd be a real knee-slapper. Elliot quickly brushed off the thought.

Ms. James continued, "Let me tell you, young man, I've seen her with my own eyes. And it's true what they say: those who do wrong go to less pleasant realms of the spiritual world."

"What does that even mean?" Elliot asked skeptically.

Ms. James choked back a tear. "Well, I'll tell you my story. It's been well over thirty-three years, and I still remember it as if it happened yesterday." Ms. James began to story tell.

"On a gloomy autumn day, my sister Esther and I were headed to the old library on Manor Road. It's unfortunate to see it abandoned now, especially after all the beautiful memories my sister and I had there."

Ms. James' voice tinged with anticipation as she shared, "Visiting the library was truly an enchanting experience for me and Esther. Every Saturday afternoon held the promise of something magical. The librarians knew us so well they would greet us by our names. 'Good day, Juliet and Esther. Have you read any exciting books lately?' they'd ask. Esther was just a year younger than I, but she always seemed smaller in my eyes," Ms. James sighed softly. "That afternoon, I stumbled upon a peculiar book on one of the shelves. It had an air of mystique and enchantment. The book's dark condition and the peculiar, foxed pages made it even more intriguing; it was truly a unique find. Little did I know that within its pages lay powerful spells. The book possessed such a magical essence, beckoning me to uncover its mystical knowledge. So, I took it home and studied it along with Esther. We then started our journey to becoming the first witches in our town, casting spells and spreading positive energy everywhere. Esther practiced spells for love, while I practiced spells for fortune. It was a wonderful time. Both seasoned witches in our mid-20s, we embarked on a journey of love and fulfillment. Soon, Esther's heart yearned for a settled life and a loving partner. She set her sights on our charming neighbor, Dimitri Evergreen, who seemed to possess all the qualities she desired in a man at the time. With a sacred ritual of romance, Esther quickly made Dimitri her groom, granting her deepest wishes. I hoped she would find true contentment once she became Mrs. Evergreen, but it was not meant to be."

"What do you mean?" Elliot asked, intrigued by the tale.

Ms. James hesitated, then proceeded, "Esther fell into something far worse than I could have imagined: deception. Dimitri soon shattered her trust when he was caught in bed with his mistress. It completely ruined their bond. Feeling adrift and filled with despair, Esther felt compelled to take matters into her own hands. That worthless scoundrel Dimitri dared to say that my sister's love no longer fulfilled his needs. He deceived Esther's heart, but the book of spells brought her even greater deception. Esther was convinced from the beginning that the incantation would forge an unbreakable love between them, but it didn't. She handed me a peculiar book shrouded in darkness on one fateful night, exuding an eerie aura."

"Was it another spell book?" Elliot asked.

Ms. James interjected, "By no means. This was no ordinary spell book. That night, Esther stormed in—she smelled of rain and night. She said no words and, with a grin, handed it to me. There were symmetrical symbols all over it. I pressed my fingers gently onto its covering and tried but couldn't interpret any of its symbols. My hands grew cold, and I could sense something evil waiting to emerge from its pages. I opened the book very slowly, and its pages whispered secrets of a sinister nature, drawing me into its captivating depth. The cursed book was adorned with wicked and devilish magic, capable of wreaking havoc upon one's existence. It instilled an ever-growing terror within me, causing my fear to intensify."

Chapter 9

Curse of the Succubus

At once, Juliet slammed the book shut. "Have you gone mad, Esther?"

Esther snatched the book back from Juliet's hands. "Oh, Juliet, why are you such a wretch?" She clucked her tongue.

"We don't dabble with what's inside there," Juliet said, pointing to the book. "You must get rid of it."

"No!" Esther glowered at Juliet—the room filled with a deafening silence.

"You need to tell me where you got that book," Juliet demanded.

"What does it matter? This book holds the key to all my questions. You don't need to worry," Esther said, turning her back to Juliet.

Juliet's eyes widened with fear, "You have no idea what you're getting into. Delving into the unknown can lead to serious consequences."

Esther scowled at Juliet. "Well, I don't see it that way."

Juliet fell to her knees, her voice trembling as she begged, "Esther, it is not a book of good spells. It's a book of malediction, and it's downright diabolical. You should have it removed from your possession at once," Juliet sucked in a breath before lifting herself from the ground. "I demand you return it to where you found it. The book can be destructive when not used cautiously. It does not belong here."

Esther scoffed, "You really believe I lack caution?" Esther's words dripped with a sardonic tone.

"You-you are cautious," Juliet stammered.

Esther let out an eerie chuckle, "You know what I think?" Esther began to stride around the room. "The power of jealousy speaks volumes." Esther's voice took on a whole new tone. It was as if she had unlocked a dark power within her. "I've finally figured a way to get Dimitri back into my arms, and you're trying to stop me. Is it because you never knew love yourself, sister?" her lips curled into a crooked smile. "Can't you see? This book is my pathfinder, Juliet!" Esther said as tears filled her dark brown eyes. "It holds the key to my pain, erasing the hatred in my heart for a man I once loved." With an evil grin, she revealed her cunning plan. "I'll invoke the captivating spirit of Belladonna," Esther said with a smirk. "My appearance will be imbued with irresistible beauty, sensuality, and attraction, capturing Dimitri's heart ultimately. Dimitri will rue the day he ever laid his gaze upon another woman. As my transformation will leave him longing for me once more."

Juliet gasped in horror, "Esther, please . . . you don't have to do this." She begged.

"I have to do this!" Esther shouted, her face flushed with anger. Suddenly, a soft and low chuckle escaped her lips. She narrowed her eyes at Juliet. "It's not over," Esther spoke softly. Clutching the book tightly in her hands, her eyes circled the room momentarily before she bolted out the front door and into the wet, desolate streets.

Juliet's voice echoed through the street as she cried out, "Come back!" but it was too late. Esther disappeared into the shadowed night.

Ms. James returned her attention to Elliot. "After that, the days grew cold and dreary. Blind to the curse, the townsfolk failed to see the fierce spiritual battle before us. I knew what lay ahead, but the people were unprepared for the impending chaos that came next."

Chapter 10

Knock! Knock!

"It was a cold September night when an abrupt knock came at my door, awakening me from my —" Ms. James' continued, her voice trailed off with static.

"Esther had returned, but she was almost unrecognizable," Ms. James' voice was unsteady. Elliot drew his attention closer. "I'm sorry, Ms. James. I think there's an issue with your connection."

Suddenly, the static stopped. Elliot waited to hear Ms. James's voice again.

"Are you still there?" He asked. No answer.

Suddenly, a deep growl came through the phone, interrupting the call. Hairs stood up on Elliot's back.

"Hello? Ms. James, are you there?" Elliot yelled, his voice cracking.

He pulled the phone closer, but there was silence on the other end. Ms. James was gone.

How could Ms. James leave me on edge? Maybe I should call her back and check if she is okay. He thought.

Elliot's pulse quickened when a soft knock sounded at his front door. He froze in place. His arms tensed at his sides as he listened, not breathing. His heart skipped a beat as he realized his mistake again- forgetting to lock the door.

"I knew there was something important I forgot to do." He took in a deep breath.

"Who's there?" Elliot shouted from the kitchen. He paused, awaiting a response. He peeped his head out from the kitchen into the dark hallway that led to the front door. He then heard a muffled scratching sound at the door. "Ahh, it's probably that pesky fox again. It's been coming to our doorstep every night." He sighed and headed for the front door, dragging his feet on the wooden floorboards.

Suddenly, another knock came at the door again. This time, the sound came louder than the first.

Knock, knock!

Elliot paused, "That's definitely not a fox." He said out loud.

Knock, knock! Echoed throughout the house again.

"All right, all right, I'm coming!" Elliot shouted; he sped up his pace toward the door.

The knocking continued. **Knock! Knock! Knock!**

Elliot shook his head in frustration. He got to the door and swung it open.

"Would you quit—" His words cut short. His eyes widened to find there was no one. He slowly stepped a foot outside and poked his head out.

Am I hearing things?

His eyes searched the front yard, but there was no hint that anyone was around.

"Seriously, who was that?" he said out loud, his voice filled with curiosity.

Elliot turned, but before he stepped back inside, he noticed an abnormal mark on the front door. "What the—?" He narrowed his eyes at the door and realized that whatever had done this was certainly no fox. The scrapes were not light but deeply engraved into the wooden door. Something was trying to get inside.

"Damnit! Elliot sighed heavily and stepped back inside the house. He closed the door shut. The house was silent. He stood inside the doorway momentarily when something caught his eye. A shadow figure stood just a few feet ahead, almost like the one he had seen in his truck that night. The dark figure stood by the door that led downstairs to his bedroom.

Elliot swallowed a lump in his throat and blinked, trying to bring it into focus.

The shadow had two glowing red eyes that glared as it moved carefully. It appeared to take the form of a woman— he could tell by its feminine curves.

"Who-who is there?" He stammered. His eyes fixed on the specter, waiting for a reply. No answer. He examined the figure from where he stood; it seemed to move closer. "This whole thing is just friggin' nuts!" He exclaimed, suddenly dashing towards the shadow, which instantly disappeared. Elliot whirled around. There was no one there.

He glanced around the hallway, his eyes slowly adjusting to the darkness.

Is it possible that everything was just a figment of my imagination? Or could it be that eerie story about Ms. James and her sister haunting me? He wondered.

He looked down at his bare feet that stood cold on the wooden floor.

Curious about Esther, he shifted back to Ms. James's story.

I wonder what happened to Esther.

He chuckled to himself. "Well, if Ms. James really wanted to finish her story, she would call back, right?"

Although Elliot's mind raced with unanswered questions, he knew he would have to face them soon.

Chapter 11

The Invitation

It was October 1st, and the sky was covered in dull gray clouds, blocking the sun's warm rays. Elliot's recent days had been devoid of paranormal encounters, and the strange events surrounding him had faded from his mind. The apartment viewing with Belladonna had come to a standstill, and the memory of Ms. James and her story slowly slipped away. Yet, a lingering curiosity remained as he often wondered about her.

Devon, just like Elliot, decided to put a pause on his apartment search. He chose to stay on campus for another semester but still took the opportunity to visit and stay with his parents on the weekends. Elliot put most of his time into the auto shop. He had just been promoted to supervisor, which entailed long hours and no time for distractions. Life seemed to settle back into its familiar rhythm.

It was a Friday, almost closing time at the shop, when Sammy asked, "Staying late again today?"

Elliot nodded, "Yes, boss, just killing time like a pro. Maybe I'll take another customer."

Sammy was the shop manager. He was a stubby man with a shaved head and a mustache that twisted upwards. He walked with a limp and appeared to be around his mid-fifties.

Sammy briefly paused before he replied, "All right. Got any big plans for the weekend?" he asked.

Elliot chuckled, "Well, my buddy Devon is in town for the weekend. I'm sure we'll find something to do."

Sammy nodded, "You mean the Owens boy? He's a great kid!"

Given the intimate nature of a small town, it is no surprise that Sammy would know the Owens family.

Sammy jingled his car keys and said, "Well, I'm heading home to the missus. You boys, stay safe this weekend." Sammy motioned to the exit door.

"Sure thing, I'll catch you on Monday," Elliot smiled.

"Oh, and *don't* call me if you need anything," Sammy said with a husky laugh.

The doorbell chimed as he made his exit. Elliot pulled out a chair and plopped down behind his desk, and just when he thought he had a moment to himself, his phone pinged with a notification. Curious, he picked it up and saw a new message in his inbox. He checked the message where he discovered an invitation to a weekend party.

"OCTOBER'S HORROR FESTIVAL," it read in big, bold letters.

"By order of all goblins and ghouls, you are hereby summoned to attend our spine-tingling celebration of thirty-one nights of Halloween, starting this Saturday and every weekend until Halloween!"

It was an exciting surprise that added a touch of anticipation to his day.

"This is going to be epic!" Elliot said out loud.

He glanced at his wristwatch, stood up from his chair, and grabbed the keys to his truck. "I've got to tell Devon."

Just as he was about to wrap up at the shop, the doorbell chimed, signaling the arrival of an unexpected customer.

"Is this a bad time?" a gentle female voice called.

Chapter 12

Goddess

Elliot gazed intensely as the woman entered the shop.

"I apologize if this is bad timing, but I thought I could get a second pair of eyes to look at my car. There's this unstable noise. I assume it's the engine." She giggled and gave a gentle smile.

Elliot stood in admiration of her good looks. She was beautiful, with chiseled features, long brunette hair, and a striking physique.

Elliot continued to stare, speechless.

Say something. Anything! His conscience scolded.

Elliot snapped his sagging jaw shut. "I-I can take a look at that," he stammered, rushing to the door. "Please, after you." He gestured a hand, waving her ahead of him.

Her eyes steadily locked with Elliot's.

Elliot had never seen such captivating eyes before.

She must be a goddess. He thought.

She flicked her hair and crossed her arms, "Hopefully, it's an easy fix."

"Well, let's find out," Elliot asserted as they approached her car. He anchored the hood open and placed a hand on his hip, his eyes trying not to wander to the stunning stranger but instead staying focused on his work. "Ahh, I see the problem here," he said, leaning closer for a better look.

"What is it?" She walked over to Elliot's side, her arms still crossed. The wind danced in her hair.

Elliot pointed out, "See, the fan blades here. They need to be replaced." Elliot didn't realize how close she stood, her elbow rubbing softly on his.

"Okay, how much is it going to cost me?" She placed a finger over her pink lips flirtatiously and bit them gently.

Elliot watched; his mouth gaped. "Oh, this one's on the house," he said as he wiped sweaty palms on his pants, swallowing a lump in his throat.

"No charge? How generous of you." She winked at Elliot.

Elliot nodded. The sides of his mouth turned up in a warm smile, and a red flush warmed his cheeks. There was an awkward silence after he realized he'd been smiling too hard.

"So, are you new around here?" he asked, breaking the silence. "I've lived here my whole life and never seen you around before," Elliot asked, interested in her answer.

The woman let out a sly smirk, "I'm not. Just here for work."

"Sweet! So, what's your line of work?" he asked.

"Oh, I don't think you want to know." She put a hand on his shoulder.

"I'm all ears." He replied.

"Well, let's just say it's kind of. . . I don't know, complicated? God, I've already said too much." She looked down shyly and brought her eyes up to Elliot. "Shall we get this fixed?" she pointed at the car.

"Right. I have to run inside and grab the new fan blades. This shouldn't take long; I'll be right back." He turned and headed into the shop.

The woman's breathtaking beauty couldn't escape Elliot's mind. She was flawless, like a dream come true, and carried herself with sartorial elegance. He had to uncover her mystery.

"Maybe I should ask her out," he mumbled aloud.

Inside the shop, he rummaged through a few boxes piled on one another.

He suddenly had a brilliant plan, "I know! I'll invite her to the Halloween party this weekend," he plotted. "What's the worst that could happen—she'd say no?" he chuckled.

"This should be easy," he thought.

"Ah-ha! Here it is." He placed the fans under his arm and headed out front.

Outside, the woman appeared frazzled. She slammed down the car's hood, her eyes darting around the area, scouting. "I've got to go. I'm so sorry." She glanced over her shoulder to see Elliot's confused expression as she hopped into her car.

"Is everything okay?" he asked.

She rolled down her window. "Yes, something important has come up."

"Will you be back? You really should switch out those blades," Elliot affirmed with concern.

"I'll try to return as soon as possible," she grinned.

Elliot stood like he had been star-struck. "Okay," he said.

Her gaze fixated on Elliot, her eyes locked in intense focus before saying, "Elliot. This might be a little straightforward, but I must say, you are one *very* handsome man." She fluttered her eyes, casting a spell of allure that left Elliot mesmerized.

"I'm-I'm flattered," Elliot stammered.

"Pardon my next remark, but has anyone ever told you how good you smell?"

"How good I smell? No. I think you're the first," Elliot laughed.

"Well, then. It's good to know that I'm your first." She rolled her eyes playfully, "I'll be back very soon." The woman let out an ear-to-ear smile. "I should get going," she started her car.

Now's your chance. Ask her out, Elliot scolded himself.

"Hey, would you want to go to a Halloween party . . . tomorrow night?" Elliot blurted.

"Halloween party? But it's only the first week of October," she replied.

She pondered momentarily, "Come to think of it, I could never say no to an early Halloween celebration. Where's this party happening?"

"The location is right on Manor Road," Elliot said.

The woman's eyes widened with a knowing expression, "Manor Road. Ah yes, isn't that where the old, abandoned library is?" the woman asked.

"Oddly enough, that's where all the fun goes down. The library has been remolded and turned into a club," he chuckled.

"So, is that a yes?" Elliot asked with anticipation.

"You can count me in." She let out a little giggle.

Elliot's eyes lit up with excitement. "Great! The party starts at nine o'clock."

"I'll wear my best costume just for you, Elliot." She gave a wink and drove off.

Chapter 13

She's Dead!

Elliot closed the shop and went to Devon's house as the sun dipped below the horizon. On his way, he passed Ms. James's house and noticed an ambulance parked outside.

He pulled his truck into the Owens's parking garage and took a moment to contemplate.

God, I hope Ms. James is okay. He thought.

His phone pinged as he swung open the truck's door and stepped onto the rocker panel. It was a notification—a new inbox message.

He read out loud in a whisper:

> Hello, Elliot.
> Long time no hear! I wanted to remind you that my offer for that fantastic rental still stands. It was just renovated, and I must say, it is something to DIE for. If you're interested, I can set up a quick tour.
> – Belladonna

Elliot pondered the offer, feeling more inclined to accept it now. He eagerly anticipated a fresh start, ready to leave behind the Belladonna tales of Ms. James and Devon.

Elliot: Hello, Belladonna,
Does Sunday at noon work?

Before placing the phone into his pocket, it pinged again. Belladonna replied expeditiously.

Sunday at noon works just fine. Oh, and please remember, NO visitors are welcome during the tour. I'll call you with more details in a few.
Belladonna

Elliot: Not a problem. I'm looking forward to meeting with you then.

Elliot let out a deep sigh and walked toward the front entrance of Devon's house. Just as he stretched out a hand to knock, the door opened.

"Elliot!" A startled Devon clamored while taking a step back. "I was just about to call you. Come inside." Elliot could see the sadness in Devon's eyes.

"Have you checked your phone? I've been calling you all afternoon." Devon stared at Elliot.

"No. I never got any missed calls from you," Elliot replied, "What's the matter?"

At that moment, Mrs. Owens burst into the room.

"Oh, Elliot!" Mrs. Owens bawled as she rushed to his side. Mr. Owens trailed behind her, hands jammed in his pockets and his head lowered, moving slowly.

Mrs. Owens looked up at Elliot and squeezed him tightly. "Isn't it awful? We—" Mrs. Owens's voice struggled with tears. "Oh, I need a tissue." She stepped back, her words brief.

"What's going on?" Elliot insisted.

"Haven't you heard?" Mr. Owens asked in a low, firm voice.

"Heard what? No one's told me anything. . . is it my dad?" Elliot glanced wide-eyed at Mr. Owens.

Mr. Owens shook his head no, removing the glasses on his face. "It's not your dad. I was actually on the phone with him just now, breaking the terrible news."

Elliot stood, waiting for a response, "What news? Is anyone going to tell me what's going on?"

"It's Ms. James," Devon said, his voice low.

Elliot raised an eyebrow. "What about Ms. James?"

"There's no other way to say this. . ." Devon paused.

"She's dead!"

Chapter 14

An Unsolved Mystery

"Dead! How is that possible?" Elliot shook his head in disbelief, "I was on the phone with her not long ago."

"Wait a minute, you spoke to her?" Devon asked, lifting his head.

"Yeah, she called me a few weeks back—." Elliot's jaw clenched.

Do not mention Ms. James story. They'll think I'm crazy. Elliot thought to himself.

"Was there any mention of her feeling unsafe or being pursued by someone?" Mrs. Owens asked. Elliot could hear her sniffing back a sob.

Elliot hesitated, "Nothing like that. She just apologized for dialing the wrong number and hung up."

Elliot paused for a moment. He couldn't wrap his head around the news.

"Was it late at night when she called you?" Mr. Owens asked.

"I can't remember," Elliot lied.

"The cops are questioning everyone in the neighborhood," Devon said.

Elliot's face was masked with confusion, "Questioning? Why?"

"They're suspecting a murder," Devon said.

"Murder. But-but how?" Elliot stammered.

Mrs. Owens cried, "Oh, it's just horrible!"

There was a deathly silence in the room.

"I'm afraid there's no other way to say this, but she was discovered strangled by her telephone cord," Mr. Owens explained.

Elliot took a step back, "Jesus . . ."

"It gets worse," Devon added.

Mrs. Owens's face crumpled with sorrow as she sobbed, "Oh. I can't bear to hear it again," She quickly rushed upstairs to her bedroom, covering her ears.

Elliot glanced at Devon, who kept his head down. He waited to hear something. . . anything.

"Her tongue . . ." Devon's voice broke. "It was gone."

"No!" Elliot gasped in disbelief.

Suddenly, Elliot's ears filled with the sound of ringing.

Who could be responsible for such a brutal and horrifying murder?

Elliot shook his head in disbelief. "Are you sure about this?" his eyes turned to Devon with concern.

"At least, that's what we've been told," Devon replied.

The silence in the room was so loud it seemed to fill every corner.

Elliot's eyes widened in utter disbelief. "Have they found the person who did this?" he asked.

Mr. Owens shook his head, "We do not know," he replied. "Strangely, there was no sign of an intruder. It's an open investigation. He said eyebrows crossed. "Ms. James never bothered anybody in this town. I don't know what would possess someone to do such a thing to such a sweet lady," Mr. Owens's disappointment was visible.

"How long ago did this happen?" Elliot asked.

"We just found out later this afternoon. But they're predicting she'd been dead for maybe weeks." Mr. Owens said, his eyes filled with tears.

"I can't believe this," Elliot said, his eyes wandering around the room. "There's got to be someone out there who knows or saw something. This is heavy news; I-I think I should go." Elliot stammered.

"I understand," Mr. Owens said, nodding his head.

"Where are you going?" Devon asked.

"I need to find out what happened," Elliot said, opening the door and leaving.

Devon tailed, "We just told you—she was murdered."

"Yes, but someone is responsible," Elliot hurried to Ms. James' house.

Devon hesitated to follow while Elliot walked ahead. He then quickened his steps to catch up with Elliot. "Are you crazy?" Why are you suddenly so concerned? You made fun of Ms. James for years." Devon said in a sarcastic tone.

Elliot stopped in his tracks. "I did, and that's where I was wrong." He snapped.

"People like Ms. James are no different than the rest of us. This neighborhood ostracized her because they did not care to understand a poor old lady. Don't you feel a little guilt from that, too?"

Devon's eyes widened. "I do." Devon paused, speechless. "So, what are you going to do about it? Devon asked.

"Get answers! Ms. James could not have died the way she did. I'm going to find out what really happened, and no one will stop me."

Chapter 15

Body bag

Elliot and Devon continued to the front of Ms. James' house. Caution tape was wrapped all around her front yard and porch. Reality suddenly hit.

Ms. James really was gone.

Police officers were on the scene, and sirens were approaching the neighborhood from the streets away.

Elliot and Devon watched silently across the street.

Devon paused before speaking, "Oh no," His gaze remained fixed on the house, his eyes locked in a steady stare of disbelief. The more he stared, the creepier it got. Instantly, the front door opened.

It was Ms. James, unfortunately. The only way out of her home was in a body bag.

Elliot and Devon watched in disbelief as forensic investigators escorted her body into an ambulance. The scene made them shudder.

"You boys shouldn't be here," one cop shouted, advancing toward the two.

Devon and Elliot turned their eyes to the cop in a blank stare and slowly turned back to Ms. James' body.

"Did you boys hear me?" The officer scolded. "This is a crime scene. I need you guys away from the area. Now!" The cop's hands waved in a circular motion.

"What happened?" Elliot questioned.

"It's an open investigation. We need this area cleared. Let's move it!"

"Yes, officer." Elliot turned and began to walk away back to Devon's house.

"I can't believe we just saw Ms. James being carried out in a body bag," Devon said, walking a couple of steps ahead of Elliot. "This neighborhood has officially lost its mind. Suddenly, there's a killer on the loose. What if one of us is next!" Devon exclaimed.

Questions filled Elliot's thoughts again.

What if the night the phone went dead was the night she'd been murdered?

They moved further away from the crime scene and back to Devon's house. When they arrived, they sat slumped on the front steps of Devon's porch. The air filled with quiet.

"What do you think about all this?" Devon asked, raising an eyebrow.

Elliot huffed and opened his mouth to utter a word, but Devon cut in before he could.

"I think it's time I share something with you."

"Okay, go ahead." Elliot sat up sharply.

Devon cleared his throat, "I thought I'd gone completely bonkers after the whole spiel with Belladonna."

Elliot turned his eyes to Devon.

Devon's eyes lit up as he said, "The inbox messages, the unknown calls, it was all overwhelming. But then, snap! It all vanished. It sounds crazy, but I owe it all to Ms. James."

Elliot gave a quizzical stare. "What do you mean you owe it all to her?"

Devon paused momentarily, gathering his thoughts before speaking again, "She gave me a ring for protection, and I think it's a natural guardian. Devon stretched out his hand, eagerly showing Elliot the ring on his finger.

Devon took a deep breath and continued, "Unique, isn't it?" The ring emitted a radiant glow.

"At first, I'd been skeptical about accepting something from Ms. James, but it really did save me."

Elliot glanced at the ring intensely, "I've never seen a ring shine this way. You'd think it was enchanted or something," Elliot said, his eyes squinting.

Devon let out a soft chuckle. "It is enchanted. It's an onyx, and it protected me from Belladonna."

Elliot stood entranced by the lustrous ring.

Devon pulled back his hand, no longer showcasing the ring, "Well, that's my little memory of Ms. James. I should probably go inside and break the news to Samara." Devon stood up and turned, ready to push the front door open.

"Wait," Elliot called from over his shoulder.

Devon stopped with his back facing Elliot and turned slowly to face him.

"I want to know more of what you know. I also want to know what really happened to you in the back seat of my truck that night," Elliot said.

"I know you saw something," Elliot anticipated.

Devon stood quiet for a long moment.

Elliot stood up from the front porch steps, his eyes peered at Devon. "Come on, Devon, we've always had a bond built on trust and honesty, like brothers. Let's wipe the slate clean and start fresh. No more fabricated stories anymore. I want to know the truth."

There was a long pause before Devon stared at the onyx ring on his finger absently. He took it off, rolled it back and forth between his thumb and index finger, and then put it back on. He took a deep breath and said, "All right. I promise to tell you everything if you do the same."

Chapter 16

Devon's Truth

As the stars dimmed, the streets became cloaked in an enigmatic fog. It was an eerie sight.

"I think it might rain. We should probably take this conversation inside," Devon said.

Elliot settled down on the steps, "I think we're okay out here," he leaned forward, placed both elbows on his knees, and gestured for Devon to sit beside him.

Devon paused, digging his hands into his pockets, and replied, "No thanks. I'm good standing," he sighed long, "So, you're finally serious about hearing the truth, huh? Well, it's far worse than you can imagine." Devon explained, "I might sound like a broken record, but Belladonna is not who I thought she was. She's not an ordinary being." Devon held nothing back this time, creating an atmosphere of suspense. He continued, "She possesses these supernatural abilities, truthfully. With a hint of fear, Devon paused and exclaimed, "She's a succubus!"

Elliot caught his breath and stared at Devon.

Devon proceeded, "It doesn't matter to me if anyone, including you, believes what I say. I know this to be true because I fell right into her diabolical trap; it was a terrifying experience, and that's what I was trying to warn about that night in your truck."

Elliot's eyes held unwavering trust in Devon's words, "You mean to tell me you were up against a demonic entity the entire time?" he glanced up sharply, his brows furrowed.

Devon replied with certainty, "Yes, and that so-called apartment is nothing but a feeding ground. She lures people in there to finish them off."

Elliot interrupted, "What do you mean by finish them off?"

Devon gave Elliot a long, hard stare, "You know exactly what I mean."

Elliot's voice quivered, "So, you believe she's taken lives in that very place?"

Devon nodded, "I know for a fact she is," his voice cracked. He swallowed back a tide of emotion, "It's like she feeds off their life force. It's-it's horrifying," he stammered.

Elliot stood up and slowly walked toward Devon. He took a deep sigh and placed a hand on Devon's shoulder. "I believe it," he said.

Devon shook his head, "Hmm, and why now? You only pretended to believe me the last time. Why suddenly the change of mind?"

Elliot explained, "I know this might sound a bit off the wall, but I believe you because of Ms. James," he said calmly.

"Hold on, are you only convinced because of Ms. James' death?" Devon exclaimed, clearly flustered.

Elliot seemed a bit conflicted, "Yes, I mean no. The night Ms. James called me, she shared this bone-chilling story of her sister, Esther, who invoked the entity of a spirit called Belladonna. According to Ms. James, the entity is described as a wicked and seductive spirit with unparalleled beauty and power to control one's fate. Perhaps the Belladonna you know and met is the same one Ms. James warned me about, and she's still at large."

Devon nodded. "You could be on to something there." He could feel the weight of Elliot's gaze, indicating that he was dead serious.

"So, after all this time, you're actually a believer?" Devon laughed to himself in disbelief.

Elliot nodded firmly, admitting, "I can't deny it now, even if I wanted to. Your story and Ms. James' story seem to match. It can't be a random coincidence. I haven't told you this, but lately, I've felt a looming darkness following me since I got involved with Belladonna. I'm starting to believe that everything is somehow connected. So, to answer your question, yes. This is what's made me a believer."

Devon took a step back, "Wait a minute. What do you mean by involved?"

"Belladonna and I have had phone conversations, and I planned to meet her this Sunday," Elliot whispered.

Tension filled the air before Devon replied, "You mean to tell me you're still considering meeting her?" Devon's eyes glazed in a deep stare, "After Ms. James warned you that Belladonna could very well be the demon that's possessed her sister, Esther, and then tried to kill me? How many people with the same name, Belladonna, do we know? Not even one, right?" He snatched Elliot by the shoulders and said, "Please don't do it. You do not want to see what I saw!" Devon's eyes dilated with terror.

There was a moment of silence while they stared fixedly at one another. Elliot shrugged his shoulders and tried to utter a word but couldn't. Elliot could see Devon's fear, causing them to turn away, unable to maintain eye contact.

"Let's go together," Elliot blurted out.

Devon spun back to Elliot in full rage. "Are you out of your mind!" he shoved Elliot. "There's no way I'm ever going back there."

Elliot pointed at the onyx ring on Devon's finger, "What about the onyx ring? Didn't you say it saved your life?"

Devon brought the ring on his finger to his eyes, "Yes. It shielded me from that demon."

Elliot suggested, "OK, what if we give it another shot together and send her back to where she came from? We can find a way to break the curse. It's what Ms. James would've wanted, right?"

Thoughts raced through Devon's head, weighing the risks and uncertainties. He questioned if he had the strength to face such a powerful and manipulative entity again, fearing the consequences it could bring. However, deep down, Devon wanted his own revenge. With a determined look, he took a deep breath and said, "Let's do it!"

With relief flooding him, Elliot's eyes lit up as he approached Devon. Their palms met in a firm, reassuring grip, symbolizing their determination to face the daunting challenge of confronting Belladonna.

"Our first plan is to act like nothing's out of the ordinary and go to this Halloween party tomorrow night," Elliot said.

"Halloween party? But it's the beginning of October," Devon scoffed.

Elliot rolled his eyes, "Dude. Halloween, party, and booze. Who would turn down that combination?

Devon excitedly replied, "I guess it's not such a bad idea."

Elliot exclaimed, "Hell, it's not! This party is going down every weekend for the rest of the month. Doors open at 9 p.m. Bring Samara; don't forget to dress up. I also invited a hot date for the occasion," Elliot let out a soft chuckle, "You and I are going to play it cool, and afterward, we'll have enough liquid courage to face Belladonna. What do you say?" Elliot's face lit up with a wide smile.

Devon took a deep breath. His mind wrapped around the actuality that Elliot had finally come around and believed everything.

"I'm on board," Devon replied, "But under one condition," Devon looked into Elliot's eyes. "Samara and anyone else joining us for tomorrow's party stays out of it. Deal?"

Elliot nodded, "Deal! I won't put anyone else in harm's way. I'll make sure our dates are safe at their homes before we make our way to Belladonna," Elliot declared, his tone filled with determination.

Elliot's voice trailed off as he entered his truck. "I'll call you tomorrow," he said, turning the engine on.

Lifting a finger on his left hand to say goodbye, Devon's heart filled with uncertainty as he watched Elliot drive off.

Chapter 17

The Break In

Elliot rounded the corner of a dimly lit street that revealed Ms. James' house in a short distance. The neighborhood was now clear of the ambulance and police cars. He drove his truck to the front of her home for a better look. The house lights were off, and there was no sign of anyone inside. He reversed his truck and parallel-parked.

"Am I really about to do this?" His jaw tightened.

Everything about Ms. James's death bothered Elliot.

"I know there's got to be more answers about Ms. James, Esther, and Belladonna inside the house."

Elliot leaped out of his truck and scouted the street for any passersby. He could hear the barking of dogs in the distance. He made his way to the front of the house with a sense of urgency, fixing a piercing gaze upon the aged, decrepit structure. An eerie silence settled over what was now considered a crime scene. A small fence surrounded the front yard, short enough for Elliot to step a foot over. Glancing over his shoulder, Elliot looked for any sign of the police, but all was clear. He stepped one foot over the fence and into Ms. James's front yard. A cold chill instantly ran up his spine, raising the hairs on his neck. Taking one more look around, he lifted another leg. He was in. Yellow caution tape was wrapped around the entire front porch. Elliot ducked down and moved swiftly and stealthily toward the back of the house. Suddenly, without noticing, he stepped on the tail of a stray black cat lying on the ground. The cat let out an intense yowl, turned to Elliot, and hissed before running across the street. Slightly terrified, Elliot hurried his way to the back of the house. Leaves crunched under his feet as he tiptoed quickly toward a double-hung window on the house's side.

"I can get in through here."

The window was at eye level. He quickly peeked inside and saw nothing unusual, just plain darkness. With a struggle, he opened the window, sprung up using all his upper strength, and climbed in. Inside, he collapsed onto dusty wooden floors, falling on his right side.

"Ow!" he cried, grabbing onto his shoulder tightly. He lifted himself from the ground and glanced around the dark house. The air was filled with the unmistakable aroma of a dank, musty basement. He swiftly retrieved his cell phone from his pocket and activated the flashlight feature as he inspected the home for clues. The bobbing light reflected off a small mirror lined up on a back door, frightening Elliot momentarily.

"Holy Sh—! Oh, it's just my reflection," he chuckled nervously.

Elliot grew nervous, but he also felt a rush of excitement. He approached the mirrored door and opened it with hesitancy. The next room was the kitchen, where Elliot flashed the light on a half-full cup of tea and a moldy muffin sitting on the kitchen table. He turned the light over to the house phone on the kitchen counter.

Ms. James mentioned something about a spell book. What if that book is hidden somewhere in this house? What if it has answers? Elliot thought.

Scavenging the kitchen drawers, Elliot found nothing. Silverware clattered as he opened one drawer after the next. Not finding any clues, he took a deep breath. He flashed the cell phone's light around the kitchen, finding a door leading to another room. It was decorated with photographs.

He squinted through the dim light, reaching for one particular photo. It was a ferrotype photograph of two young women. Elliot drew the phone's light closer for a clearer look. He gently pulled the blurry picture from the door, which was fixed with a gluey paste. Curious, he turned the photo over. The back read, "Juliet and Esther, 1960."

Sweat stung his eyes, and he wiped his face with his sleeve. The photo showed Ms. James and her sister, Esther, standing in a cornfield in front of an old Victorian home. The sisters appeared to be in their early twenties. Ms. James, the taller one, wore an elegant solid-color turndown-collar swing dress, while Juliet wore a polka-dot smock dress. The sisters posed, hugging one another, cheek to cheek, with bright smiles. Their flipped bob hairstyles captured the essence of the 1960s.

Suddenly, Elliot heard heavy footsteps coming up the creaking front porch stairs.

He quickly tucked the photo into his back pocket, clicked off the phone's flashlight, and peered blindly through the dark for a way out. Within seconds, he found the open window in the room he had first entered.

"I bet someone caught sight of the open window."

Elliot could hear fiddling with the doorknob. Someone was trying to get into the house. Elliot darted toward the window, striking his foot on an old rocking chair's edge and falling to the ground. He crawled to the window, stretching out a hand to the windowsill. He attempted to lift his body off the ground, but a cold draft entered the room at that moment. The front door was now open, meaning someone was inside the house.

Chapter 18

Intruder

The shard of moonlight through the open window made the room dull gray. Elliot glanced around, spotting a sofa draped in a quilt. He swiftly crawled to hide behind it. Once there, he pressed himself against it, trying to steady his breath. The front door slammed shut as footsteps approached, but suddenly, they stopped.

There was an uncanny silence. A cold sweat broke out on Elliot's forehead, and he mopped it away with his forearm.

He could hear the footsteps recede and enter the room opposite—the kitchen.

His attention dropped to the floor.

"They'll catch me if I run now."

Elliot's eyes shifted toward the window and back to where he stood.

"I can hide myself underneath the sofa." Quickly lifting the drape, Elliot crawled slowly and carefully underneath the sofa. Then, at once, he heard rapid and loud footsteps coming to where he was.

The heavy footsteps echoed in the silence until they grew closer in the same room. Elliot held his breath and closed his eyes without making any sudden movements. What he heard next left him trembling in fear. A deep snarl vibrated the wooden floors. He could hear the unmistakable sound of an animal sniffing the air. Whatever it was, it sounded large based on its weighty footfalls. Elliot opened his eyes and glanced around for anything he could use as a weapon. He spotted what appeared to be a black set-top box under the sofa by him, an arm's reach away.

Cautiously, Elliot reached for it and realized it wasn't a set-top box but a book.

"Could this possibly be the book of spells?"

Elliot kept his shaky hand on the mysterious text, bemused. The intruder had to be part human, part beast, as it let out a low growl that rumbled the room. Suddenly, the sound of a cell phone rang.

God, please don't let that be my phone. Elliot hoped.

Luckily, it wasn't his phone that rang, but the strangers. The stranger let out a grunt before answering.

"I'm in," the intruder said, with a gruff, masculine voice, turning to leave the room.

Elliot stood frozen from any sudden motion. His heart filled with anxiety, causing slight palpitations.

Paused under the sofa, he eavesdropped on the stranger's conversation from the next room.

"This is my second time coming here. I've checked the shelves and the basement—everywhere, both upstairs and downstairs. Nothing." The stranger gave a deep sigh. "I told you. It isn't here. We'll never get our hands on it!" he snapped.

Elliot swallowed a lump in his throat and blinked with surprise. His eyes turned directly to the book.

This book has got to be what he's looking for. Elliot thought, with a satisfied smirk on his face.

The stranger continued, "Unless…you think it was passed on to someone else? Perhaps to one of your *lover* boys." The strange man let out an insidious laugh. "By the way, have you heard from our next target?" The man's voice boomed and rattled the floorboards as he spoke.

"Who could he possibly be talking to? Elliot's mind raced with curiosity, wondering who might be on the other end of the mysterious conversation.

The stranger proceeded, "Yes, tomorrow night is perfect. It'll be quite the feast, indeed," the stranger exclaimed with a bone-chilling tone.

The footsteps became faint before the front door opened and slammed shut. The stranger was gone. Elliot waited in silence, staring at the floor. He emerged from under the sofa, his body moving sluggishly in the quiet house. He stood up, brushing away the dust that stuck to his clothes with one hand and holding the book in the other. He quickly climbed out the window. Touching down onto the grass, Elliot bolted to his truck and swung open the door. Flinging the book to the passenger seat, he leaped behind the steering wheel and sped off.

Chapter 19

Whispers in the Dark

It was almost midnight when Elliot arrived home. He grabbed the book and hurried inside.

"Dad, I'm home!" Elliot shouted.

He paused to think about his thrilling experience at Ms. James's house. He clenched the book with both hands. There was undoubtedly more to Ms. James's story; since the book was now in his possession, he could learn all about her kept secrets. He removed his shoes and tossed them beside the doorway.

"I said, I'm home!" He waited for a response, but there was none.

With the book in hand, he went down a small hallway to the kitchen. He switched on the kitchen lights and turned to a sink of unwashed dishes.

"I guess he's still at work," he said out loud.

He put the book and cell phone on the counter, pulled a fresh, cold can of beer from the refrigerator, and cracked it open. Pulling out a chair, he took a seat at the dinner table. He reached for the book and placed it on his lap. Before opening its pages, he remembered the photograph of the two sisters tucked in his back pocket. He pulled the photo and slid it into one of the book's pages. He chugged his beer, letting out a loud belch, and wiped his mouth with his wrist. Opening the first page, he realized it was Ms. James's journal, not a spell book. The journal chronicled every significant moment in her life. Elliot flicked through the journal pages when a second photo fell face-down onto the floor. He could see faint lettering on its back—a date, 'Manor Road, 1961.' Reaching for the picture, he turned it over to glimpse a young woman in a wedding dress; it didn't appear to be Ms. James.

"This may be Esther."

The photo wasn't clear enough, although she looked much like the young Esther in the first photo. But the more Elliot studied the picture, the more familiar the woman's face seemed, as if he had met her.

"Where have I seen you?" he tried recollecting.

His cell phone suddenly rang, sending a jolt of surprise through him. He looked and saw the call was from an unknown number.

Without hesitation, he answered on the second ring, "Hello?"

There was a slight pause before an unrecognizable voice answered,

"Beware the shadows that dwell in the abyss, for they guard secrets that shall devour your very essence."

Elliot threw the phone to the ground and shot right up from his seat, the journal and photo landing on the floor. He glanced around the room with frightened eyes. He raced around into the next room, his heart pounding. He aggressively flipped on the lights throughout the house, room by room, his senses heightened as he listened for any sounds of an intruder. Silence all around. Mopping sweat off his forehead, he walked back into the kitchen and picked up his belongings from the ground.

"This night's getting a little too weird." He scoffed.

Just as he was about to head to his room, a familiar tune came from his downstairs bedroom.

Elliot swallowed a lump in his throat and slowly made his way downstairs.

As he descended the final step, a gray-white light emanated from his computer screen, casting ethereal shadows throughout the room.

"Unknown caller would like to FaceTime," displayed across the monitor. Elliot stepped in front of the computer that sat on a small desk. Holding the journal, he placed it by his side and answered the Facetime. The other end of the call was dark. Elliot brought his face closer to the screen, "Who's there?" Elliot waited for someone to reveal themself.

There was an imperceptible whisper in the background. It almost sounded like someone calling his name.

He drew an ear closer.

"Elliot!" a hoarse voice called. In seconds, the camera zoomed in to a horrifying, distorted face.

Chapter 20

Dark Magic

Elliot sprang backward, nearly losing his footing.

The caller steadied their camera.

"It's me. Devon," he said, his eyes filled with intensity.

Elliot pulled the swivel chair from underneath the desk and sank onto it, his face masked in relief. "You couldn't call me on my cell?"

"I did, but it went straight to voicemail," Devon murmured.

Elliot checked his phone log for any calls. There were none.

"Why are you up this late?" Elliot asked.

"I couldn't sleep. I kept thinking, and you're absolutely right. Ms. James's death caught us all off guard. I needed to find answers of my own." Devon's eyes wandered away from the screen.

Elliot 's eyes locked onto the screen, "Wait. Are you—?"

Devon nodded, turning the camera around and showing Elliot a dark room.

"Mhm, I'm inside Ms. James's house."

The words burst from Elliot's mouth, "You need to get out of there!"

"Oh, come on. You said yourself you wanted to get to the bottom of things. Why don't I take the lead and start it off for you?" Devon flipped the camera view back to himself.

Elliot could see there was a shadow figure that lurked around Devon. It moved slowly.

"Devon—watch out!" Elliot's voice rang out sharply.

Devon's eyes darted around, scanning the surroundings, "What is it?"

Elliot pointed, "There's someone behind you!"

Devon switched the camera view and faced it behind him. "Oh, you mean her," Devon focused on the dark figure and zoomed in.

The shadowed figure turned around and walked closer to the camera light. It was Samara.

Elliot sighed deeply, "How on earth did you guys manage to get inside?"

Devon turned his eyes to Elliot, "We got in through an open window on the side of the house. Anyway, I've got some more crazy stuff to tell you. Do you want to come meet us?" Devon reversed the camera back to himself.

"I-I was actually just there," Elliot stammered. "I managed to sneak inside after our talk. Listen, it's not safe where you are."

Devon could hear the worry in Elliot's voice. "Is 'The Elliot Vargas' afraid?" Devon let out a sarcastic laugh.

"Shh. You're too loud," Samara chimed in.

"All right, all right," Devon nodded. "So, you won't believe what Samara told me about Ms. James," Devon continued.

Elliot rubbed his forehead with two hands, dragging them down to his face. "What could Samara possibly know?"

With a sense of urgency, Devon replied, "A lot! It turns out that Ms. James and her sister practiced witchcraft."

"Keep your voice down, or we're going to get caught," Samara called from a distance.

"Okay, I'll hush," Devon lowered his tone.

Elliot leaned back in his chair, eagerly tuning in to every word.

Devon continued, "Hold on tight because this story is wild! When Esther conjured what she thought was a benign spirit—to help her get back at her cheating husband, Dimitri, not only did her spell work, and she got her wishes to come true, but Esther tried to break off the pact with the entity. But the spirit had more plans in store for its vessel. Soon after Esther disappeared, her ex-husband was discovered in their home, covered in strange bite marks. Investigators found his body had been completely drained of blood. There are suspicions that the spirit possessed Esther to do this, and once Esther realized the damage she caused, she vanished without a trace."

A period of quietness now set in. "So, how does Samara know all of this?" Elliot asked.

"Her grandmother. She knew Dimitri's mistress. In the end, everyone started thinking the mistress had gone mad. So, over time, the story transformed into a small-town legend passed down to their children and then, their children's children, kind of like folklore."

Devon paused and listened intently for a few seconds, "Did you hear that?"

Holding his breath, Elliot tried to get a better look through the screen. "I can't see anything from this side. What is it?" He asked.

Devon strained his eyes in the darkness.

Elliot whispered, "What are you staring at?" he asked, afraid to know.

Devon sucked in a quick breath and met Elliot's gaze steadily. "Nothing. I thought I heard something."

Elliot let out a breath of relief. "You two shouldn't be there. There's been someone checking in on the house."

"Oh, that's right. You would know that information because you came here without us," Devon said sarcastically.

Elliot glanced up and rolled his eyes.

Devon laughed, "I'm kidding. So, what did you find when you were here? All I see is a bunch of old furniture. There's also this unrecognizable odor," Devon's face twisted funnily.

Elliot chuckled. "I didn't find much, just some old photos clustered on the kitchen door. Oh, and her journal."

Devon paused, "You found Ms. James' journal!" he exclaimed in surprise.

"Yes. I haven't read through it just yet," Elliot reached for the journal beside him and brought it to the screen.

"Dude, there's got to be so many answers in there. But wait a minute, I think its pages are falling apart," Devon pointed.

Elliot turned his eyes to the book, "Oh, that's just a couple of pictures I tucked inside," Elliot could see the photograph of the two sisters slipping through the journal's pages. He removed the photos using two fingers and presented one to Devon.

"Voilà! Behold the legendary sisters, Esther and Juliet," he presented the photograph, "Aye, Esther looks kind of hot in this picture, right?" Elliot tittered. "Wait a minute. I figured it out: the more I look at the photo, the more Esther reminds me of the girl I met at the shop—except for the old-time hairdo and gown, that is. Did I tell you about the girl I met at the shop?" Elliot babbled on.

Devon stared in mute silence—a look of terror on his face.

Elliot lowered the photo from the camera. "All right, I get it. You don't find her appealing," Elliot shrugged his shoulders.

Devon clamped a hand over his mouth.

"What is it? Did I say something wrong?" Elliot asked with suspicion.

"It can't be," Devon said, shaking his head.

"That's . . . that's . . . her!" There was a tremor in Devon's voice.

"Yes, it's Esther," Elliot reassured.

Elliot stared at Devon, confused. He raised an eyebrow and drew the photo in for a closer look.

Devon stood pointing at the women in the photo and exclaimed,

"No. Elliot, that's Belladonna!"

Chapter 21

The Escape

Elliot stared at the photo one last time in disbelief; he couldn't utter a word.

"This would mean Belladonna was secretly disguising herself, mingling amongst us, in Esther's body."

Suddenly, Devon and Samara heard a car engine revving down the street.

"Devon, did you catch that?" Samara asked, tuning in to the sound.

"Someone's coming! We need to get out of here now," Samara yelled.

The car engine fell silent. They held their breath, waiting in anticipation.

"Guys, hurry up!" Elliot exclaimed.

The two made a run for it. The camera shook in Devon's hand.

"There's the window!" Samara shouted.

Elliot's eyes blazed with intensity as he rose from his chair, making it hard to see what was happening. "Did you guys make it out already?" he asked, trying to ease the panic.

"Ow!" Samara screamed from a distance. "Help me!" she cried out.

The phone dropped outside and onto the ground. The camera landed, facing the house, the picture somewhat blurry. The moonlight caught the corner of Elliot's eye, where he spotted Samara darting away from the home and out of the camera's view. Devon struggled to free Samara's denim jacket caught in the window ledge.

He gripped onto the jacket one last time, but no luck. He could hear footsteps approaching, creating panic.

"Forget the damn jacket!" Samara said in a breathy voice.

Elliot could still see the jacket hanging from the window ledge. He glanced at Devon.

"Bro, just leave it!" Elliot yelled.

Devon turned his head in both directions and dashed toward the cell phone, picking it off the ground.

"We made it out!" he exclaimed as he raced down the street with Samara.

"You guys are incredibly brave," Elliot cheered.

Devon and Samara laughed, slowing their pace.

"Phew, that was too close," Devon said, trying to catch his breath. "Oh, and Elliot, don't forget. We need a ride to the big party tomorrow."

Elliot nodded. "You got it. I'll see you loonies tomorrow."

The face call ended.

Elliot's mind wandered back to Esther.

"Perhaps it's worth giving Ms. James' house another look. Maybe I'll find the coveted spell book this time," Elliot grabbed Ms. James' journal and dived into a page at random.

September 23

Oh, Esther, my heart aches for you, dear sister. Where have your true self and spirit gone? I remember looking into your once bright and vibrant eyes, but now they are void of life. I will not let the entity win. Please come back to me.

Elliot shut the journal and placed it on his nightstand. This journal didn't seem to include any spells or provide him with any answers to break the curse.

He wondered if any form of protection could also keep him safe from Belladonna's reach, just like the onyx ring did for Devon.

He tried to quiet his racing thoughts and drifted into a deep slumber.

Chapter 22

The Ritual

With the room plunged into an unsettling darkness, Elliot slipped into sleep paralysis. He attempted to move, but his body remained unresponsive. His chest heaved up and down. His eyes wandered around the room as he tried to let out a scream for help but couldn't.

"Is this a dream?" he thought.

Abruptly, the bedroom door swung open, and a strange green mist lit the room. Elliot watched breathlessly. From the corner of his eye, a shimmering apparition stood at his bedroom door. Its shadowy form strode toward Elliot and stopped at the side of his bed. Sweat dripped down his forehead. Unable to utter a word, Elliot spoke with his thoughts.

"Who are you?"

The figure hovered over his side, lowering its head at Elliot's motionless body sprawled out on the bed. The figure drew closer, where it manifested itself in a faint glow.

"Ms. James? You're alive!" Elliot eyes widened. Somehow, she could read Elliot's mind, and without speaking a word, she nodded yes.

Elliot's lips froze in a grimace, "I can't move. Please help me," Elliot begged.

At that moment, she placed her hands on Elliot's temples and chanted. "*Tempus praeteritum*," she shouted, circling her arms towards the ceiling.

The ground shook, and a sudden wind howled through the room, causing a stir.

In an instant, Elliot's body levitated above his bed. His eyes rolled back as he was suddenly transported to a mesmerizing old Victorian house, alone in a seemingly endless hallway. Sunlight streamed through tall glass windows ahead, emitting a golden glow to mildewed walls. Elliot had traveled back in time.

"This place. I think I know it", he thought. His bare feet were cold, standing on the hardwood floors.

"Hello!" he yelled, "This is the same house in the picture that stood behind Ms. James and her sister in the photo."

Out of nowhere, the anguished cry of someone in pain resounded through the entire house.

Elliot listened intently, "Is someone there?" His efforts to get a response were futile.

The pitiful wailing came from upstairs. "Does someone need help?" Elliot asked, rushing up the staircase.

In an instant, Elliot's eyes widened in disbelief as he discovered a youthful and lively Ms. James, just like the one he had seen in the photograph.

She cried in the fetal position, her head buried in her knees.

Elliot approached with caution, extending a hand.

Her sobbing suddenly stopped. She slowly lifted her head; her face looked grim. Her eyes were puffy and bloodshot. She let her gaze fall sternly at Elliot as she shook her head, pointing a finger ahead to a room further down the hallway.

"There," she said in a cracked voice.

With an intense and focused gaze, Elliot turned his eyes toward the foreboding darkness of the hallway. "What's down there?" he asked, his voice filled with concern.

Ms. James' eyes remained fixed on a door hidden in a dark shade. She whimpered for a few moments and directed her attention back to Elliot.

"You must go inside and stop her!" she begged.

With unwavering certainty, Elliot was convinced that Ms. James was referring to Esther. "Do you know how I can vanquish Belladonna? He waited impatiently for an answer.

She failed to grasp his question, burying her face in tears.

Elliot glanced at the door and tiptoed toward it. He raised a hand to knock, but the door opened on its own. Suddenly, a mysterious force pulled his body inside fast. The door slammed shut. Breathing heavily, Elliot glanced around the room. Sunshine leaked through cracks in the window blinds, making light patterns in a room filled with exotic plants unlike any Elliot had seen.

"Plants thrive when you provide them with good ground, sunlight, and natural nutrients," a soft feminine voice echoed around the room.

Elliot drew a shaky breath, "Who said that?"

A seemingly young Esther suddenly appeared from behind a collection of Atropa belladonna. Dressed in dark clothing, she revealed her slim figure. She closed the curtains, shutting out the light and her face remained concealed. She then modeled one of the peculiar plants in front of an elliptical mirror and began to pick at it. Elliot leaned in for a closer look and saw what appeared to be berries stacked in a bowl.

"Esther?" he said, clearing his throat. "Don't do this."

Esther's stoic expression gave no attention to Elliot. She kneeled to the ground and smiled at her shadowy mirror reflection. Lighting three pillar candles, she began to hum quietly.

Elliot watched as she reached for a dark book by her side.

"The Book of Curses! The one Ms. James spoke of!" Elliot gasped.

This was not a greenhouse; this was an altar, and Elliot was placed right in the middle of a ritual.

She opened a page of the book and began the spell:

> "Come to me beyond the sphere.
>> I call to you, rid my despair.
>>> Prepossess my dull appeal.
>>>> Turn me, Belladonna.
>>>>> Reveal. Reveal."

Elliot's pulse pounded like a drum in his ears.

"Wait a minute, the belladonna plant is also known as the deadly nightshade. It's poisonous! Now Esther is about to consume its deadly berries to seal her deal." his eyes filled with fear and disbelief.

At that moment, Esther grabbed a handful of berries from the bowl and squeezed their black juices into a jeweled chalice, continuing her chant:

"With this, I consume all parts of thee into my stream.
Take your place as I devour thy poisonous seeds.
Belladonna, I intake thee. Latch onto me.
Everlasting beauty overtake me."

Esther brought the chalice to her mouth and drank.

"No!" Elliot shouted, darting toward her. With his attempt to stop the spell, a force immediately dangled his body in the air and rammed him against a wall. Esther's body lay sprawled on the ground, her mouth smeared with the thick black fluid.

"Esther, stop!" Elliot shouted, grunting as he struggled to escape the force that bound him. Finally, he broke free and fell to the ground. It was now too late. The entity schemed its way to have Esther's soul forever.

The room suddenly plunged into complete darkness; Elliot couldn't see through the thickness of gloom. He heard a woman's short laughter from behind, followed by a legion of whispers in his ears. A loud whoosh of what sounded like wings went past him.

All at once, a dim light flashed at the exit door. Elliot raced to it, pulling on the door's handle, but it was locked. He banged on it frantically.

"Let me out of here!" He yelled.

An eerie quiet followed, and then a low growl made his body tremble.

"I'll help you . . . if you help me," a gentle female voice said. Footsteps approached.

Struck by the voice behind, Elliot cried out, "Never!" Shaking, he turned slowly to face the voice from over his shoulder. A look of horror crossed his face as he watched soulless eyes staring at him intensely. A deep, rumbling snarl gave away the human-looking creature; it was the succubus. Her eyes were red, her skin gray, and her lips dry. Gooey black fluid dripped down from her chin to her cleavage. She wiped it away with her hand and gave an evil grin. Sweat crept down the back of Elliot's neck.

"What do you want from me?" Elliot's voice trembled with fear.

The succubus drew nearer. She pressed her fingers gently over Elliot's brows, tracing down to his lips and chin. Elliot let out a deep sigh through his nostrils.

She then glowered at Elliot, with eyes as red as burning coals, and pulled him close, baring her sharp teeth, and replied, "All of you," she said in a demonic voice.

Elliot shut his eyes tightly and screamed, "Help me!" Right away, he felt his body sink. He awakened with a gasp, his body jolted upright. He thrust back into the familiarity of his room. Relieved, Elliot let out a long breath.

At that moment, his phone rang—an unknown caller.

He answered in a panic after the first ring. "Hello?"

Suddenly, a loud growl entered the line, alarming Elliot before he instantly hung up.

His phone rang a second time, startling him. He let it ring several times before answering,

"Leave me alone!" he bellowed.

Devon's voice came through the line, confused, "Elliot, is everything okay?"

"Oh, Devon, what's going on?" Elliot chuckled nervously.

Devon scoffed, "What do you mean what's going on? Did you forget what today is?"

Elliot took a sharp breath, feeling disoriented, "I don't have the foggiest clue," he said.

"It's the night of the Halloween party, remember?" Devon said with a hint of annoyance.

Elliot grunted, "No. That's tomorrow night.".

"What do you mean it's tomorrow night?" Devon said sarcastically, "Today is Saturday, and it's already seven-thirty," Devon laughed.

Elliot immediately leaped out of bed, "No way!"

Devon cackled. "I've been calling you all day."

"That would mean I was asleep for nearly the entire day?"

Devon laughed harder, "Yeah, it looks that way. It must've been one heck of a nap! Anyway, Samara and I are just about ready. Are we still carpooling?"

Elliot let out a frustrated sigh, "Sure, sure. . . . I'll be on my way soon. I just have to hurry up now," Elliot said and hung up the call.

Astounded, Elliot couldn't believe Ms. James had appeared to him in a revelation.

"I'm really curious about who gave Esther the book of curses?" he stood puzzled.

Giving a sidelong glance, Elliot swiftly snatched the journal and began skimming for answers through its pages.

"Ugh, I can barely make out any of this. The handwriting is too crowded."

He paused and ran a frustrated hand through his hair.

Come on, there's got to be something.

Finally, he flipped to its final pages. With trembling hands, he held the journal up high to his gaze and focused on the crammed words, his eyes dazzled by the first words: "Breaking the curse of Belladonna."

"Jackpot!"

Chapter 23

Breaking the Curse

"I can't believe it! I finally found the answer to break the curse," Elliot exclaimed, his voice filled with astonishment.

Suddenly, his phone rang. The number was unknown.

"Hello, who is this?" he answered sternly. He was sure he could hear slow and heavy breathing.

"Enough with the crank calls!" he shouted angrily, abruptly ending the call.

To quickly distract himself, he turned on some music and put together a costume. Soon enough, he was ready to go. He headed upstairs when he heard tires crunching on gravel outside.

Elliot watched as his dad pulled into the driveway.

"And where have you been?" Elliot called out.

Mr. Vargas scoffed, "Looking for you. Don't you answer your phone anymore?" he replied. He shot Elliot a piercing gaze, his eyes scanning him from head to toe as he sat in his car.

"And where do you think you're headed, looking like someone out of an 80s horror movie?" he added while exiting the car.

"It's for a Halloween party," Elliot replied.

Mr. Vargas shook his head, "Nice try, buddy! Halloween isn't until later this month," he sneered sarcastically.

"I guess they're getting a head start on the festivities this time," Elliot laughed.

Mr. Vargas rolled his eyes, "Ahh, you young folk always find any reason to party." He said, shaking his head.

He approached Elliot for a better look at the costume. He rested a hand on Elliot's shoulder, motioned to the house's entrance, and paused before saying, "Elliot, you know I don't hover, but it would be nice for you to check in sometimes. You're my only kid, you had me worried," he sighed, "I checked your room, and you weren't there. I shouted your name a few times throughout the house, and there was no answer. So, I took a drive down to your workplace. The guys said you were off today, so I returned to check here again. Thank goodness you're okay," Mr. Vargas looked over his shoulder to be sure Elliot was listening. He turned around and began to fiddle with his house keys. His eyes peered at the side of the door.

"Damnit! Did that fox scratch up this door again? This is the third time this week!" he yelled in frustration.

Elliot calmly explained, "Dad. I'm sorry. See, my phone has been acting a little weird," he said sincerely, "Also, what do you mean I wasn't in my room? I've been sleeping in all day."

Mr. Vargas studied Elliot for a moment and grunted.

"Come on, Dad. You have to believe me. Maybe you were dialing the wrong Elliot," he said jokingly.

"Oh, I'm old, but not that old." His dad gave him a sarcastic smile.

Elliot chuckled, opening his truck's door. "I'm heading out tonight. You might not want to wait up for me."

Mr. Vargas couldn't help but shake his head, clearly exasperated, "Oh, by the way, rumors are spreading around that you have a new girlfriend?"

Elliot's gaze locked onto his dad's face, "I do not have a girlfriend. Trust me, you'd be the first to know," Elliot replied from his truck while the door stood open.

"Well, that's not what I heard," Mr. Vargas said, his tone filled with suspicion. "The boys at the shop told me a young lady has been down there asking for you."

Elliot paused, allowing his thoughts to settle, "Ah, so she did end up coming back after all," he said with a mix of surprise in his voice, "I-I mean, she's just a customer from yesterday, no big deal," Elliot stammered.

Mr. Vargas nodded. "Anyway, I've got the rest of the night off, so I'll be home."

"All right, Dad," Elliot said and started the engine.

Mr. Vargas waved a hand, "Hey, son?" he called out.

Elliot rolled down the truck window, "What's up?"

"Be careful out there," he said, his voice dripping with a warning, "Things can get a little strange around this time of year," his tone quieted Elliot.

"I'll be okay, Dad. There's no need to worry," Elliot replied before driving away.

It was dark when Elliot approached Devon's house. He pulled the truck to a curbside when his phone rang—another unknown number. Elliot answered anyway.

An alluring female voice came through the line before he could speak, "Elliot, are you there?"

Elliot hesitated to answer, "Yes, who's calling?"

She replied, "You invited me to a party tonight, remember? I jotted down your number from one of the guys at the shop. I hope you don't mind."

There was an awkward silence.

"Are you still there?"

Elliot squeezed his eyes shut, hoping to give himself courage, "Yes, I'm here."

The woman gave a calm reply, "I was hoping you were still on for that party?"

Elliot guaranteed, "I sure am."

She shouted excitedly, "Great! I happen to know the venue like the back of my hand. Just keep your eyes peeled for the edgy lady rocking the devil horns," she said in a playful and flirtatious tone.

"Devil horns? Sounds pretty wicked already," Elliot chuckled at the intrigue.

"I won't be too hard to miss," she said in a whispered voice.

Elliot blushed and let out a short laugh.

"Oh! I almost forgot!" she gasped, excited, "I invited my brother, Zagan. He loves Halloween just as much as I do. I hope it's not a problem."

"Sweet, that's not a problem," Elliot assured.

"Well, I'll catch you there," she said before hanging up.

Elliot sighed in relief, "I still didn't catch her name."

Suddenly, A loud bang hit the window. Elliot gasped for a moment and steadied himself. His eyes turned over to the right-side-view mirror and then the left. No one was there. He did a double take when he spotted a man's silhouette by his truck. The man sported a top hat and a dark tailcoat jacket with a face painted like a skull.

Elliot attempted to flee in his truck before the gearshift stubbornly jammed.

"Ugh, come on!" Elliot shouted.

The man swiftly made his way to the passenger side and forcefully struck the driver-side window with a single hand.

Elliot shouted fiercely, "Back off from my truck!"

The man remained silent, his gaze fixed on Elliot, a perpetual grin stretched across his face.

Terrified, Elliot leaned forward, igniting the engine, and forcefully shifted the gear into motion. He prepared to speed away when the man's voice pierced through the truck's window, "Chill out, it's just me!"

Suddenly, Elliot realized the stranger's voice.

"Devon!" Elliot shrieked, raising both eyebrows in shock.

Devon threw his head back and laughed, breaking free from his costume character.

Elliot's eyes flared, "Dammit! It is you. You got me so damn good this time!" He laughed nervously.

Devon laughed even harder, "I wish you could've seen the look on your face!"

Elliot shook his head and motioned for Devon to hop in the passenger seat.

"How did you know I was outside?" Elliot asked.

"Anyone could hear you and that roaring truck from miles away," Devon replied sarcastically.

Elliot rolled his eyes. "So, what are you supposed to be, some kind of stylish skeleton?"

"Uh-uh, I'm a witch doctor," Devon said, grinning right in Elliot's face.

Elliot scoffed. "You're probably going to freak people out tonight."

"That's the whole point, right?" Devon's voice cracked.

"Mind if I spill my guts?" Elliot asked.

"Let it out," Devon nodded.

Elliot inhaled sharply, feeling the weight of everything that needed to be shared, "The past couple of days have been a total nightmare. It's mind-boggling how we've become entwined with an entity from the past, haunting us through the depths of the internet. It's like a real-life horror movie," Elliot said, leaning back in his seat.

Devon sighed frustratedly, "Listen, it all makes sense why Belladonna hasn't stopped. In today's society, we're missing out on face-to-face connections due to the impact of technology. And guess what? Belladonna is no exception to this. She has been around for a while, so it's no wonder she's using any means necessary to achieve her desires. It's all about adapting to get what she wants. These low-vibrational entities can be cunning, as they've learned to stay up-to-date with their tactics. They can disguise themselves and shapeshift. They can meet you in your dreams. Sometimes, they can even be your next-door neighbor. The thought of what they can do sends shivers down my spine," Devon sucked in a deep breath and continued. "I'm just relieved you came around this time and believe it's real now. Belladonna has no means to back down. Her reaching out to you proves that. She seems trapped in this eternal limbo, consumed by the idea of unfinished business, and somehow, she's still latched onto Esther's body, using it as a vessel to prolong her presence. But it's time to put that vessel to rest."

There stood a moment of silence, shrouded in an eerie stillness.

Devon removed the onyx ring from his finger, "Here. It would be best if you held onto this since she's after you now," he said, placing the ring gently into Elliot's palm.

"I can't take your ring. Then she'll come after you again."

"You're right," Devon sneered, lowering his head. "The question I keep asking is, why us?"

With a stern tone, Elliot replied, "Well, according to legends, succubus targets young men like us to drain our life force or energy. It's their way of survival. As you mentioned the other day, they feed on the essence of one's soul. Belladonna couldn't take Dimitri's soul, so she drained the blood from his body. And now, she's hellbent on revenge because she couldn't get yours either. She's out for blood and soul."

Elliot smirked, "But I've cracked the code," he whispered. His gaze filled with intensity and focus. "I found that the only way to truly vanquish the succubus for good is by forcing her to glimpse at her own reflection."

Devon's eyebrows crossed, "Her reflection?"

Elliot dug under his seat and handed Ms. James' journal to Devon.

"Go on ahead and check the last page," he urged.

Devon flipped to its last page. "Is this really her journal?" he asked as his eyes scanned the writing on the page. The words read,

> "After extensive research, I've discovered the solution to break the curse. One must get the entity to see itself in a magical reflector. The mirror's power will instantly consume her essence. Once captured, shatter the glass to seal her defeat once and for all. Regretfully, I lack all the courage to undertake this task, for I can only see my sister, Esther, imprisoned in a realm of darkness and despair. I am not strong enough to see beyond a carnal image. I'm simply not capable enough to break the curse."

"So, this means Belladonna is still alive because Ms. James couldn't confront extinguishing her own sister's life."

Elliot nodded, "Yes, Ms. James, with a heart full of dread, could only think of her beloved sister, Esther. She couldn't follow through with breaking the spell. That would have meant killing her own sister."

Devon turned his eyes to Elliot. "But what about the onyx Ms. James gave me? Is it any good?"

Elliot explained, "It is, but it seems like the ring was crafted to maintain a safe distance from Belladonna. It can't fully vanquish her. That's why she remains on the hunt."

"Well, where can the magical mirror be found?" Devon asked.

Elliot pondered, "We never got a chance to check the attic. I have a feeling it's somewhere in that house," he said, lifting a brow.

"We also never got to check the basement," Devon added.

"It can be anywhere around the house," Elliot paused, "We must go back to Ms. James' house tonight. It's the only way."

"But what about returning to face Belladonna?" Devon questioned.

After giving it some thought, Elliot suggested, "How about we mix things up? We start by heading to Ms. James' house after the party and search for the mirror. Then, we confront Belladonna at the apartment. Sound like a plan?" Devon nodded in agreement, "Sounds like one very long night," he laughed, "but it actually sounds like a great plan."

Suddenly, another bang struck Elliot's truck from behind. Elliot and Devon jumped up and quickly turned their eyes to the back.

"Oh, it's just Samara!" Devon said, grabbing onto his chest.

"Ha-ha! Your faces were absolutely priceless!" Samara exclaimed with enthusiasm.

She snapped a whip over the side of the truck, "Like my circus whip?" A slow smile worked its way across her face. She opened the truck's door and dropped into the back seat.

"Just a friendly reminder, we're already one hour behind schedule," Her pigtails danced with the slightest head movement.

"We know that now. Great costume, by the way. I take it you're a—" Elliot pretended to guess.

"Ringmaster!" Samara cut in, her eyes lighting up mischievously.

"All right, then. Let's get this show on the road!" Elliot shouted with excitement as he drove off.

Chapter 24

Drink Up!

It was ten o'clock, and the venue doors buzzed with loud music and vibrant energy. Samara was mesmerized by the orange-colored lights outside the club. "Wow, it sounds wild in there!" The entrance was adorned with spiderweb-inspired decorations, setting the creepy scene.

Before entering, Devon gave Elliot a little shirt tug. "Hey, do you really think it's a good call to venture to Ms. James's house tonight, out of all nights? You know, especially since we're in costume?"

Elliot turned to Devon, "Don't tell me you're getting cold feet now. You and I know the mirror is the sole solution to end all of this," he said.

Devon nodded, "You couldn't be more right. Forget I ever questioned."

The trio confidently sauntered into the club.

Inside, strobe lights colored the club walls and floors. The bartenders dressed in skimpy costumes, serving themed cocktails and shot glasses on glowing trays.

"This is so awesome!" Devon shouted excitedly over the dark wave music. He squeezed Samara's hand, and the two shared a kiss.

Elliot glanced around, searching for his date for the night. "It's too dim in here. I can't make out anyone's face."

Devon pulled in for a listen. "Are you talking to me? I can't hear you," Devon shouted, pointing to the club speakers that hung above.

Elliot shook his head. "No. I'm just thinking out loud." Elliot dug for his phone in his pocket, checking for missed calls. There were none.

"I'm an hour late. I hope she didn't leave." Elliot thought.

Elliot sucked in his breath and thought to dial her number but remembered she'd called from a private line.

"Did your date bail on you?" Samara pulled herself into their conversation.

"No. I'm going to check upstairs. Hey, why don't you guys get me a drink while I look?" Elliot shouted above the music. "I'll get the next round, I promise."

"All right, just don't get lost," Devon yelled.

Elliot jogged up the nightclub stairs decorated with tiny jack-o'-lanterns. Upstairs, he pressed himself into the vast swarm of people dancing, laughing, and shouting at one another in conversation. The loud bass vibrated the nightclub walls and floor. Elliot huddled in a cramped corner beside a fake rotted corpse skeleton sitting on the ground. He glanced around, sensing eyes piercing him from across the room. He spotted a woman standing in the shadows with a glowing smile.

She strode across the room, entering the light and the crowd.

As she got closer, Elliot spotted horns on the woman's head.

Elliot gulped at the sight, "It's her."

The woman donned a chic gothic dress, black in color, paired with captivating red boots and a meticulously crafted horned headpiece, creating an illusion so lifelike it was almost surreal. Her long black hair had a lovely gloss that gleamed under the flashing club lights.

Walking behind her was a tall, handsome man. He had a muscular build and rocked a black half-mask that covered most of his mouth. All that was noticeable were his large eyes, which were bright and snappy. He wore a long black cloak and studied Elliot intently.

The two strangers got closer to Elliot. They then lowered and raised their heads to signify their agreement.

Elliot was speechless for a moment.

"You look lonely," the woman said, smirking at Elliot. She leaned in and whispered to Elliot, "I've been waiting for you."

Elliot swallowed hard and shook his head, "I'm sorry I kept you waiting," he chuckled.

She fluttered her eyes at Elliot, "This is Zagan." The woman gestured to the man beside her. "My brother, the one I told you about."

Elliot gave Zagan a nod, "Hi, it's nice to meet you."

Zagan pulled down his mask briefly and gave Elliot a bright, charming smile before slipping his mask back over it. There was an awkward silence as the two stared sharply at Elliot, who pursed his lips and tilted his head slightly, "So, I invited some friends. I'd like for you to meet them. They're actually downstairs."

The woman glanced at Zagan as if awaiting his approval, but Zagan continued to stare at Elliot.

"Hold on just a second," the woman said.

The two had a quick private chat before the woman returned her eyes to Elliot.

"Before we meet your friends, Zagan's got a little treat for you," the woman said.

Out of nowhere, Zagan revealed a full drink from under his dark cloak, like a true magician.

"Cool trick!" Elliot smirked. He reached for the cup and pulled it to his nose, sniffing it.

"It's a whiskey mixed with—well, I can't quite put my finger on what the other scent is," Elliot said, puzzled.

Go on! Take a sip," Zagan insisted.

Elliot's eyes dropped down to the drink. He took a long gulp.

"It's time for you to catch up," the woman added.

"I love it!" Elliot exclaimed, already sweating from the drink. "I think I'm feeling a buzz."

The woman and Zagan watched Elliot with a grin on their faces.

"It would help if you two also had a drink. I can't be the only one drinking tonight. You can have some of mine," Elliot extended the cup to the woman.

"Don't worry about us. We're going to have plenty to drink tonight."

Already feeling tipsy, Elliot's words began to slur. He pointed a finger at Zagan. "What else is this drink mixed with?" He glanced at Zagan, "Never mind—you don't answer that," Elliot then turned his eyes to the woman. "When will you tell me your name?" he asked with his chin up.

The woman swiftly dismissed the question. "Oh, come on, enough chitchat. I bet you can't even finish your drink," the woman said, crossing her arms and giving Elliot a cold stare.

Elliot flashed her a grin and chugged down the remaining drink. He made a sour face and shouted, "Woo!" squeezing his eyes tight. "That one burned!" he exclaimed, opening his eyes and covering his mouth.

Zagan got closer and wiped a tear running down Elliot's cheek. "Can't take the heat?"

"No-no, I can," Elliot stammered, "This isn't crying by the way."

Elliot hastily wiped his face with both hands, his vision suddenly blurred, and his chest constricting. The woman and Zagan gazed at him as he struggled to regain his composure and catch his breath.

"Let's go. I've been patient long enough!" The woman said, tugging at Zagan's sleeve.

"Easy," Zagan said. "We need to wait."

The woman shouted, "He's faint! Anyone could see that by that. What else are we waiting for? His friends will come looking for him at any moment." She paused and looked around her.

"Just watch," Zagan said with a cold look.

Elliot stumbled over his foot, "What's with all the chatter?" His words slurred as he approached slowly, losing his balance. "Ah, I know what you're trying to do," He let out a loud belch, "You're trying to get me wasted," Elliot hiccupped.

"Yes. That's exactly what we're trying to do." Zagan turned his eyes to the woman.

Suddenly, Elliot saw the woman's face morph before his eyes, manifesting a grotesque look. Her eyes sunk deep into her sockets, and thick blood dripped down her mouth as she flashed her razor-sharp teeth.

"HOLY SH—!" Elliot screamed.

The woman smiled, her face turning back to normal. "Are you afraid?" she said with an evil grin.

"No. I-I just feel dizzy. I think it's time for me to go," he stammered, pinching his eyes shut, hoping it would clear his blurred vision.

"Wait a second," the woman said as she strode closer to Elliot. "Why don't you stay a little longer," she whispered into his ear.

Elliot took a sharp breath, "I would, but a second ago, I thought I saw you changed into some kind of demon or creature."

The woman and Zagan erupted into chilling laughter.

"What's so funny about that?" Elliot said sternly. "Ugh, just forget it. My head is spinning!" he said with a grunt. "Thank you, Zagan, for the drink, but I should really get going now." Elliot made a few steps forward and collapsed to the ground. The room began to spin. His heart thudded through his chest. He'd never experienced such a swooning sensation before in his life. "I'm all right," he said in an unsteady voice.

Zagan wrapped an arm around Elliot, pulling him to his feet. "You don't look so well. Why don't we get you out of here?"

Elliot raised his eyes to Zagan and nodded, "I think I could use some help making it down the steps," Elliot said, holding onto the railing.

"Just follow me," the woman said with a smirk. She reached for Elliot's hand and held on.

Elliot's heart raced as he glanced down and noticed a tight grip of claws around his hand. Panic surged through his body, causing him to break free abruptly. "What was that!" A scream caught in his throat.

"What was what? Are you sure you're all right?" she asked.

"Your hand . . . I saw claws," Elliot chuckled nervously.

The woman turned to Elliot. "I think your eyes are playing tricks on you. We're just getting you out of here, remember?" She gave a warm smile. "I think you've had a little too much to drink tonight." She chuckled, retaking Elliot's hand.

They continued down the steps; Zagan followed from behind.

"See, that wasn't too bad. We're at the bottom of the stairs," the woman said.

Elliot's vision was no longer blurred, and the sudden wave of weakness over his body disappeared. "I actually feel much better now."

Contemplating, Elliot took a deep breath, "That drink packed quite a punch!" he said.

"Nothing a strong man like yourself can't handle." The woman winked.

Suddenly, a voice shouted from a short distance, "Finally!"

Elliot's eyes took a few seconds to focus on the darkness inside the club. It was Samara. She'd been holding drinks in both hands.

"Ah, Samara!" Elliot tugged his hand free from the woman. He stumbled and nearly toppled off the last step, reaching Samara.

"Where were you?" She asked.

"I was upstairs. Like I said, I would be."

Samara scoffed, "I went upstairs. I didn't see you."

Elliot raised an eyebrow, "Well, I was up there the entire time."

Samara rolled her eyes, "Devon and I had to split up looking for you. Didn't think this would turn into some kind of search party."

Elliot chuckled, "I wasn't even gone long enough."

Samara corrected, "Well, it was long enough for the ice in your drink to melt." She handed Elliot a drink. "Wait a second, is that your date?" Samara pointed.

Elliot turned to see the woman and Zagan's dark shadows flickering in the flashing club lights.

"Yeah. That's her and her brother, Zagan."

Samara placed a hand on her waist, "Well, don't be rude, introduce me!" She exclaimed with a mischievous grin.

Elliot scratched the back of his head, "I will, but just so you're aware, they're a little . . . odd."

Samara shuffled her drink from one hand to the other, "It's like you don't even know me sometimes," She moved past Elliot, her shoulder brushing against his.

"Hi, I'm Samara, Elliot's friend. It's so nice to meet you." Samara stretched out a hand for a handshake.

Zagan held out his hand and gave a firm handshake.

The woman positioned herself in the shadows, blending with a part of the staircase. The horns on her head cast eerie shadows on the walls.

Intrigued, Samara leaned in closer, "You guys look awesome! What inspired these amazing costumes for tonight? They're so badass, especially your sister's. Those horns—they look so real," she said, her eyes gleaming with curiosity.

"Thank you. I'm Zagan, and, if you couldn't already tell, my sister is the underworld queen. She preys on the blood of young men." Zagan turned his eyes to Elliot and grinned. "As for me, I, too, am someone from the underworld. A collector and keeper of breath, commonly called a soul catcher."

Elliot moved beside Samara and gave a subtle pinch to her arm. He then motioned his head toward the dance floor. "Don't you have to go find Devon?" Elliot said through gritted teeth.

"In a minute. I'm trying to get to know your friends." She replied, "Anyway, you two are pretty damn wicked. I like it," Samara laughed, sipping her drink.

Zagan chuckled, "Thank you. By the way, that drink of yours looks a bit watered down. Can I offer you a special drink that'll turn your night into an experience?" he asked.

"Sure, I'll take it!" Samara nodded eagerly.

Zagan then pulled out another drink from his cloak.

"On second thought, I don't think she'll like that," Elliot darted forward, slapping the drink out of Zagan's hand.

The forceful action caused Zagan's mask to fall off his face, sliding to Samara's feet.

"Elliot, what on earth is wrong with you? Why would you do that?" she shouted.

Elliot's eyes pierced into Zagan's. "You just wouldn't be able to handle that drink."

Samara rolled her eyes and shook her head. She reached down for Zagan's mask.

"I'll get that," Zagan said, rushing quickly, but Samara had already grasped the mask.

"Here you go. I'm sorry about that. Elliot sometimes acts like a big brother." She rolled her eyes.

Purple lights flashed around them, and Samara could see Zagan's face. He snatched the mask out of her hand and put it on quickly.

The club fell into an eerie hush as if darkness had swallowed the sound.

Samara's gaze bore into Zagan's eyes. "Have we met before? Samara asked, squinting.

"I don't think so," Zagan replied.

Samara furrowed her brow, "You look familiar to me," she kept her eyes fixed on Zagan.

The club music blasted back to life, filling the dance floor with pulsating beats.

Samara laughed light-heartedly and shrugged it off, "Never mind. I think I better look for Devon now. Elliot, do you want to come with me?" She asked.

The woman joined in the conversation, "Elliot will stick around with us for a little while longer. You and your lover boy can catch us right here. We're not going anywhere," the woman said.

Samara flashed a forced grin, "Elliot, are you going to be okay?" Samara asked.

"Yes. I'm excellent," Elliot said, "Just go and tell Devon you found me."

Samara quickly pulled Elliot aside. "Where'd you meet these two?"

Elliot replied, "Well, I crossed paths with the devil lady at the shop a few days back and her brother I met today."

Samara sighed deeply, "Don't you think there's something slightly off about them?"

Elliot scoffed, "Look, I told you, they are a little odd but cool. Trust me, I'm fine," Elliot reassured.

"OK, I'll be right back. Don't go anywhere else," Samara disappeared into the crowd.

Elliot directed his attention at the mysterious lady, "So, are you finally going to tell me your name?"

The woman approached Elliot. She drew him close to her, her nose brushing over his neck. She gave a deep sniff. "You know, you're too good-looking to be asking so many questions," she said, placing a finger over Elliot's lips.

Elliot's heart throbbed with excitement.

"Should we head back to my place?" she said in a sultry voice.

"I-I wasn't aware that was even on the agenda for tonight," Elliot stammered.

"It can be," she whispered in Elliot's ear, raising the hairs on his neck.

Elliot's eyes closed in deep-rooted satisfaction.

The woman then presented him with a second drink. "Drink a little bit more," she said with a smirk, "You're so tense."

Elliot sighed heavily and reluctantly muttered, "Alright, fine," before swiftly downing his drink. He coughed a little as the strong drink burned down his throat.

"Wait a sec—I thought you were going to drink with me," he said, his eyes bearing down on the woman like a hawk.

The woman immediately became flustered. "My turn to drink is coming very soon."

Elliot could feel his phone vibrate. He pulled it out to see it was Devon calling.

"Is that your girlfriend?" the woman asked, pointing her eyes to the phone.

"No. Just my best friend calling."

"I guess I'm a lucky girl, after all." She winked.

Elliot nodded and laughed nervously. "Oh no! It's-it's happening again," Elliot stammered. He felt his body was on fire; sweat trickled down his face. "I have to get out of here." He placed his phone back into his pocket. A low moan escaped his throat.

"Now's our chance! We've got to get him out of here fast. The plan will never work if we're near the ring," Zagan said harshly.

Elliot quickly recognized Zagan's voice, "What did you just say?" he asked, his face masked in horror. It was the same voice he heard at Ms. James's house the night he snuck in. His skin flushed with goosebumps at the realization.

Immediately, everyone around Elliot seemed to move in slow motion.

A group of young men blundered through him. They were all dressed in metal masquerade masks. Feeling faint, Elliot lost his balance and fell to the ground. The group turned and burst into laughter. "Hey, watch where you're going, idiot!" one of the men shouted.

Elliot wanted to react but felt his body grow numb.

Zagan bent to the ground, threw Elliot over his shoulder, and headed for the exit.

The music suddenly seemed impossible to hear— muteness, as masked strangers stared warily.

"I'll have whatever he's drinking," a random voice shouted from the crowd.

"I can't leave my friends," Elliot sputtered.

He felt his throat tighten. He raised his head and saw the mysterious woman following. Frightened, he saw her morph again into demon form. His pulse pounded like a drum in his ear.

The woman watched as Elliot gasped.

"Who are you?" his voice quivered, sweat dripping down his chin.

The woman laughed evilly, "Oh, Elliot, I'm sure you've heard enough about me already." She reached out a hand, showing black claws. Elliot's eyes filled with terror. "My name is Belladonna," she said in a steely tone. "Here's the thing, Elliot. You made me wait long enough. So, tonight, you belong to me!" At once, Elliot felt himself thrown into the back seat of a car. As he tried to call for help, the car door suddenly slammed shut, trapping his voice inside.

Chapter 25

Captured

Inside the club, Samara continued her search through the crowd for Devon.

She sighed, "Ugh, I hate that I'm missing out on all the fun right now."

A swarm of people encircled her. They jumped and danced to the music pouring loudly from the club speakers.

"Where the heck are you, Devon?" She thought, her eyes circling the room as she pressured her way past the mob of people.

At that moment, a strong arm reached out and gripped her elbow.

"Devon!" Samara shouted, pulling Devon closer.

"I was calling you," Devon shouted over the booming music.

"You were?" She checked her pockets and gasped.

"Uh-oh! I left my phone in Elliot's truck."

"I thought so. Ugh, any sight of Elliot?" Devon asked.

"Yeah. He's by the staircase with some of his friends."

"Perfect. We should try and stay together. This party is insane," Devon grabbed Samara's hand and went to the staircase.

Shoving and squeezing their way out of the crowd, they made it to the staircase. Samara wiped her forehead, sweaty from the ambient temperature at the club.

"He's not here," Devon glanced around.

"Really? I told him not to move," Samara shook her head.

"Maybe they stepped away to the bar. What did his friends look like?" Devon asked.

"There was a guy in a black cloak. He looked familiar, and there was a woman. She had horns. I couldn't really make out her face."

Devon took out his phone, "I'll try calling him again."

"Should we step outside? It's too noisy in here," Samara suggested.

"Good idea," Devon nodded and headed toward the exit with Samara.

The phone rang four times before Devon could see Elliot answer.

Devon shouted into the phone, "Dude, where are you? We've been looking crazy for you," Devon held the phone close to his ear while pressing a finger into the other. With small steps, Samara and Devon stepped further away from the club's racket. There was no answer on Elliot's side of the call.

"Ugh. Come on, Elliot. Let us know where you are. I want to dance already," Samara yelled, her voice echoing through the streets.

Devon placed the call on speakerphone, holding it up to his chin. "Bro, this isn't funny anymore. Tell us where you are?"

Samara and Devon paused in the middle of the sidewalk and listened closely, but still no reply. Samara pulled the phone from Devon's hand.

"Now isn't the time to horse around!" She looked down at the phone, then turned her eyes to Devon, "I don't get it," she said, shaking her head and handing Devon the phone.

Suddenly, a whisper came through the line, "Devon?"

Devon could hear quiet breathing.

"Did you hear that?" Devon's eyes slowly traveled up to Samara's face.

Samara nodded, letting out a sigh of relief. "Great, he's okay. Now, can we go back inside?"

"Elliot, where are you!" Devon exclaimed.

"Help me," Elliot whimpered.

Panic gripped the back of Devon's neck.

Elliot's breathing grew rapid over the phone, "It's Belladonna. She got to me."

The phone call dropped instantly.

"Shall we head inside now?" Samara asked. She could see the look of terror on Devon's face.

Devon's breath hitched like an invisible hand tightened around his throat.

"Devon!" Samara wailed, running to him. He lurched forward a few steps before falling to the ground, his cell phone skidding across the pavement. She kneeled at his level. "What happened?"

"She's got Elliot!"

"Who's got him?" Samara asked, with worry in her eyes.

Devon exhaled forcefully, "You said you last saw him at the stairs, right?"

"Yeah, he was with his two friends," Samara nodded.

Devon turned his gaze to her. "Those were not his friends."

"What!" Samara gasped.

Devon's eyes held a serious gaze, "So, there was a guy there, too?"

"Yes, he said his name was Zagan. He offered me a drink before Elliot knocked it out of his hand."

Devon pulled himself up from the ground.

"I can't believe it, she's got an accomplice," Devon murmured. "This changes everything."

"Did-did Elliot seem intoxicated when you saw him?" Devon stammered.

"He was a little loopy."

Devon took a deep breath, "She has him right where she wants him. I have to find Elliot—he's in big trouble." Devon's eyes locked on Samara. "I promise I will make this night up to you." He slid his arms around her waist and kissed her softly.

"Make it up to me?" Samara lowered her head. "I'm going with you," she said.

Devon shook his head. "No way. This is too dangerous. I can't lose you. I'm sorry—I can't let you come."

"Stop it," Samara scolded, crossing her arms. "After what happened to you in that apartment," she grabbed Devon's hand. "You need to let me be there for you."

Devon pulled his hand away from Samara's. He paced back and forth on the pavement. There was a long silence. "Just when things seemed to go back to normal—now this," he said out loud.

"All right," Devon said firmly. "You can come. But you must follow everything I say."

"I will," Samara nodded. "Now, let's go find Elliot," Samara held a tight grip on Devon's hand.

"I think I know where he could be. We just have to find a way to get there," Devon pondered.

Samara reached into her pocket and jingled Elliot's truck keys in the air. "Elliot asked me to hold these for him before we went inside the club."

Devon's eyes widened and lit up. "Hell, yes! We'll just need to make one quick stop. There's something important I need to do first."

Chapter 26

It's Not Over!

Half-conscious, Elliot realized he was no longer in the backseat of a car. Instead, his body stood slumped against the corner of a frigid stone wall.

"Where am I?"

His heart fluttered as he blinked rapidly. It relieved the blur by a little. The darkness smelled damp; the air was still and silent.

"Is anyone there?" he said in a small whisper.

There was no one around. He thought to yell for help but remembered Belladonna and Zagan.

They'll come for me if they hear me.

Regaining his vision, he bent to his knees for a look under the door sill. A low moan escaped his throat as he focused on any sign of activity on the other side.

He thought to call Devon at that moment but realized he had no connection where he was. "Dammit—how is anyone ever going to find me?" His eyes darted from side to side.

"Think Elliot!" He depended on his inner voice to free him from this nightmare.

At that moment, he spied a small, dim light that crept under another door, suggesting there was an exit.

Elliot jumped to his feet. Staggering, he approached the door and pressed an ear against it, listening closely for any sound.

Silence.

His fingers found the door handle, and he slowly pushed it open. He stood in the doorway to see a long, empty tunnel ahead. The overhead lights flickered incessantly. He took a deep breath and took a few steps forward, his body trembling and his hands growing sweaty.

Elliot looked up to the ceiling at the flickering lights and swallowed hard, his head still feeling foggy from the drinks at the party.

Elliot whirled around to face the cellar he'd stepped out of and found the door had closed shut.

"How did the door shut?"

Elliot's heart began to race. Making a slight turn, he paused momentarily and took a deep breath.

"There's no way they'll leave me here to rot!"

He sped up his pace when inaudible whispers echoed off the hollow walls.

He paused.

His eyes circled the space. Then, the hallway turned to complete darkness. Elliot stood frozen for a moment when the lights flickered back on. They seemed to blink drastically this time. Panic and fear made his body tremble when two horrifying hands clamped onto his shoulders, thrusting him to the ground.

They dragged his body backward, pulling him back into the dark cellar. Elliot's legs kicked in the air as he fought to escape their grip.

He immediately recognized the mischievous-looking hands. They were the same ones he saw at the club earlier that night.

"Belladonna, let me go!" Elliot choked out.

The succubus continued to drag his body down the empty hallway. With arms aimlessly swinging in the air, Elliot searched for something to grab onto. His hands found the succubus's forearms and penetrated his fingernails deep into the demon's flesh.

The succubus tossed her head back, and with her mouth wide open, let out a horrifying cry before letting go and disappearing.

Elliot leaped to his feet. He turned back to see the room's door slowly creaking open. Long fingers curled around the door's panel before it swung open. Suddenly, a draft of wind blew past Elliot.

Instantly, Elliot's inner voice shouted, "RUN!"

His heart quickened as he dashed through the hallway, his footsteps sounding down the corridor. He didn't dare look back again.

"There's got to be an exit!"

Finally, there was a narrow wooden door ahead. With both arms stretched out, Elliot quickly grabbed the door handle. He pushed with all his might, finding a dark staircase leading upward.

Elliot held in a breath and bravely took a chance. He climbed his way up the stairs, skipping each step at a time. He finally reached the end to find where it led him. It was an empty apartment—no sign of anyone. The chilly indoor temperature sent goosebumps along his arms.

Suddenly, he knew where he was. . . Belladonna's feeding ground.

Elliot took his cell phone out of his pocket, still waiting for a connection.

The apartment sunk in a dark gray color. He could see flickering lights shadowed across the wooden floorboards.

"Is anyone here?" he said in a low voice.

He bolted through the apartment toward the lights and peeked his head into the room. No one was there. All he discovered was a dozen low-burning black pillar candles scattered across the floorboards. He paused to catch his breath when suddenly he heard a noise.

Click, clack. Click, clack.

The clicking noise was reminiscent of someone strutting in high heels but abruptly stopped.

"You're fast," a creaky voice said. It was Belladonna.

The hollow, empty apartment made her voice sound like she was behind him.

Elliot spun around to see there was no one there.

"But I'm faster," she said in a vicious whisper.

Sweat dripped down the side of Elliot's face to his neck. His hair was damp and matted on his forehead. "Show yourself!" he demanded.

Belladonna's laugh echoed through the room. "You were always so fearless and strong. Nothing like your weak friend, Devon."

Elliot gulped. "What do you want from me?" His eyes circled the room for the succubus.

With an evil laugh, she replied, "Just a mere vessel of flesh and soul."

With a trembling voice, Elliot replied, "You've been taunting me—I know it was you in the back seat of my truck that night. And the shadow in the hallway! I know you sent Zagan to Ms. James's house the night I was there. I know who you are!" he said firmly.

Elliot clenched his fists tight, and a prolonged silence followed.

"Think you have deciphered the depths of my being?" Belladonna giggled. "Ah, how little you truly comprehend. You see Elliot, with you, a deeper need has replaced my thirst for a human vessel. It's your soul that I crave most."

Elliot gathered his courage and let out a mighty shout, "You can't have it!"

Belladonna replied in a soft, eerie tone, "But what about your mother? I know you'd give up anything just to see her alive again."

"Leave my mother out of this!" Elliot demanded.

A perfect stillness filled the room before Elliot's phone rang. He removed the phone from his pocket. "Thank God. I found a connection. Hello?" he answered.

A familiar voice spoke. "Elliot, son, is that you?"

Elliot gaped, his face masked in shock. "Mom?" Tears stung his eyes.

"Sweetie, I'm right here with you," she said.

"Mom, is it really you?" Elliot's voice broke as a tear slid down his cheek.

Her voice was like a calming melody, "Elliot, you must give Belladonna whatever she wants. It's the only way to end all of this finally." Her voice echoed slightly with every word.

"You're asking me to surrender my soul?" Elliot swallowed hard.

"I can't!" Elliot paused, wiped his tears, and then took a deep breath. "I know you're not my mother," he said with eyebrows thick and low. "I know better than to bargain with a demon!"

An icy shrill suddenly split the air.

Dropping his phone, Elliot covered his ears when a silhouette of Belladonna appeared from the shadows just a few feet before him. Elliot's eyes widened in horror as he witnessed the gruesome sight of horns tearing out of her head. Enormous bat-like wings sprang from her body. They fluttered, and a red mist immediately engulfed the room. Quickly, Belladonna coasted toward Elliot, levitating him into the air.

Elliot stared bravely into Belladonna's red eyes as her long, sharp claws wrapped around his throat.

"I'm not scared of you!" he croaked.

Belladonna tilted her head and grinned, her razor teeth oozing with thick saliva that dripped from her mouth down her chin, drooling over Elliot like a beast ready to devour its prey.

Filled with adrenaline, Elliot contended, but it was already too late. She had him pinned against a wall.

He could feel Belladonna's hot breath on his flesh as his feet dangled in the air.

At that moment, the succubus reached for his neck to bite his flesh, but Elliot blocked her attempt with his right arm, her teeth sinking into his forearm. Elliot screamed as white-hot pain seared through his body.

Suddenly, a loud bang interfered as a door flew open, releasing a gust of dusty wind so strong it filled the room, putting out the candles.

"LET HIM GO!" a voice shouted from the darkened doorway.

Belladonna growled, dropping Elliot's body to the ground.

Elliot writhed as blood gushed from his arm. He covered the bitemark with a hand, but that did little to stop the bleeding.

The succubus slowly turned her head before crouching to the ground and growling.

"What are you doing here?" she snarled.

"You know why I'm here," the man replied as he entered the room.

Elliot's eyes adjusted to the darkness. It was Devon, and he had a tight grip on the magical mirror. Samara appeared from behind.

The succubus hissed at the sight. Fueled by rage, Belladonna lunged at them, her claws slashing through the air. Samara quickly slid the onyx ring onto her finger as Devon stood firm, wielding the reflector against the succubus.

The mirror emitted a ball of blue and white lightning, creating a force so powerful that its vigorous energy blocked the succubus from reaching Devon and Samara.

"If there is one thing about curses, they're destined to be shattered!" Devon said sternly. They watched as the mirror's supernatural force sucked the succubus right in, rocking Devon nearly off his feet.

"It worked!" Elliot's triumphant cry filled the air as the trio witnessed the succubus trapped within the mirror, crawling in feeble desperation as she vomited a thick black fluid. The succubus then let out a piercing screech, "It's not over!"

Devon scoffed, "Sure, whatever. Your time is up!" he yelled.

"Want to do the honors?" Devon asked, turning his attention to Elliot.

Elliot slowly climbed to his feet, clutching his bloodied arm, and with a limp, approached Devon.

"I guess broken mirrors don't always have to mean bad luck," Elliot said.

The reflector vibrated as the succubus let out a thunderous, diabolical scream.

Elliot gripped the mirror with two hands and crashed it to the ground. Glass shards sparkled around him.

"It's definitely over now," Elliot said with finality.

Chapter 27

Gone Forever

"I can't believe it. You found the mirror," Elliot said, catching his breath.

Devon sighed deeply, "It was in the attic this whole time, covered in cobwebs and dust."

"We found a few other things, too," Samara added.

"Wait a minute, how did you guys know where to find me?" Elliot asked, turning his eyes to Devon.

"I knew if there were anywhere she'd take you, it would be here," he replied.

"What's so special about this place anyway?" Elliot's eyes darted around the silent darkness.

Devon took a deep breath, "I don't know, but we don't have to know. She's gone now. That's all that matters." He turned his gaze to Elliot, "You might want to get that checked, by the way," Devon pointed to the bite mark on Elliot's arm.

"Oh, this?" Elliot pointed at the marks. "I'm okay, especially now that you guys are here." He gave a warm smile.

The three left the haunting chamber.

Outside, they hopped into Elliot's truck.

"Hold on there, buddy, I'll drive us home," Devon said, switching sides with Elliot.

"Home? But the night's still young?" Samara said.

"I think I should go home and tidy this wound before it gets even messier," Elliot remarked, gripping his arm.

"You're not going to transform into anything after that, are you?" Devon asked, pointing at the bite mark.

Elliot laughed. "It's a succubus bite, not a vampire bite."

Devon shrugged his shoulder, "It's kind of the same thing," Devon said jokingly.

"I'll be fine, I suppose. I'll let you know as soon as I get that bloodlust," Elliot chuckled. Devon started the engine and drove off.

"Whatever happened to that guy Belladonna was with—Zagan? Who was he?" Samara asked.

"I'm not sure, but if Belladonna is out of the picture, he's probably out too," Devon said with fingers crossed.

The trio arrived at Devon's house.

Samara hopped out of the truck and turned to Elliot. "Hey, stay out of your inbox for a while," she smiled.

Elliot chuckled, "Oh, trust me, I have a feeling I won't be checking or replying to any messages for a very long time."

Samara walked toward the entrance of the house.

Elliot turned his look to Devon. "I just want to say thank you. I would have never left there alive if it weren't for you and Samara."

Devon stared at Elliot. "I know you'd do the same for me." He paused.

"Can you believe it? We finally broke the curse. Belladonna is gone, forever," Devon said, his voice filled with amusement.

Elliot shook his head. "I still can't believe it. All of this came from a simple inbox message. I really think we should consider going back to paper mail," Devon and Elliot laughed in unison.

"I think I'm okay to drive now," Elliot said, trading places with Devon.

"Aren't you heading back to campus tomorrow?" Elliot asked.

Devon nodded, "Yeah. Before sundown."

"Would you want to meet at the Café before heading back? For old times' sake," Elliot asked with a smile.

"I'll catch you there at two o'clock," Devon said, pointing at Elliot while hurrying to Samara's side.

Elliot drove off.

Samara turned her eyes to Devon, "You think he's going to be all right?" Samara asked.

"We'll just have to wait and see."

Chapter 28

Special Delivery

The following day, Devon prepared himself for his trip back to campus.

Samara wrapped her arms around Devon, "I don't want you to go," she pouted.

Devon kissed her gently on the lips. "I'll be back before you know it, I promise."

Samara's eyes twinkled as she smiled.

"I forgot to mention, Elliot wants to meet at the café before I head on the road. Do you want to come with me?" Devon asked.

"I'd love to, but I should get home. Mom's having her book club friends over for lunch, and she needs my help setting up."

Devon pulled Samara in for a tight hug.

She buried her face into Devon's chest, "Please be careful while you're on campus," Samara said.

Devon pulled his head back and gazed at her. "You don't have to worry about Belladonna. She's done—for good," he said, kissing her forehead.

Devon pulled her in closer for a hug, his hand gently caressing her back.

"I'll walk you outside," he said.

It was early afternoon, and the sidewalk glistened from the morning rain.

"At least the rain's stopped," Samara said, heading out the door. "I must look absolutely ridiculous walking home in my costume from last night."

Devon drew Samara in and kissed her nose. "I think you look even hotter now than last night." Samara's face flushed with a rosy hue as she blushed.

"Oh, you might want to take this." Devon handed Samara a mysterious book they found in Ms. James' attic.

"You know my mom's a bit nosey around here," Devon laughed and shook his head.

"Just to be safe, keep it hidden from your family and Elliot until we learn more about it. Promise?" Devon said in a whisper.

"I promise." Samara leaned in for a kiss.

"I'll call you as soon as I get to campus," Devon said, standing in the doorway.

Samara nodded and waved goodbye. She strolled through the neighborhood to her home just a few streets down. Approaching her house, she spotted her mother outside, sitting on the porch steps.

"Well, look who decided to show up—still dressed in their Halloween clothes. Must've been a fun night," her mom said with a warm smile. Her mom wore a yellow shirt dress with a purple fringed scarf wrapped around her neck, decorated with beautiful patterns. Her dark brown hair cascaded down her shoulders like a waterfall.

"You have no idea," Samara sighed, looking down.

"Oh, but I do. You seem to forget that I was once your age," her mom said with a chuckle.

"Well . . . let's just say my adventures are probably a bit more erratic than yours were," Samara replied.

"What's that you have there? Did you go shopping?" her mom pointed at the book in Samara's hand.

"This? Oh, it's just something I left at Devon's a while ago."

Her mom grunted as she stood up from the steps. "Come on inside. Looks like my guests are dropping by early today. I got to get everything ready before they arrive," she said, turning away to enter the house.

"I'm right behind you, Mom," Samara yelled out.

"Okay, I'll start some coffee for us," her voice trailed off as the door opened slightly.

Samara paused at the front steps of the porch. She gazed up at the trees rustling in the wind—finally, some tranquility. She breathed in deeply, taking her time, and then turned around to see a package under one of the patio chairs.

"Mom, I think you got a package!" she called out.

"Oh no, honey, it's not for me. A very handsome gentleman came by and delivered it this morning. He said it was for you," her mom shouted back inside the house.

"For me?" Samara muttered under her breath. She reached for the package, then stood up, drawing it in for a closer look.

She eagerly tore open the package and was pleasantly surprised to find her jean jacket inside.

"Oh my God!" she exclaimed, her voice filled with shock. "It's my jacket. The one I left accidentally left at Ms. James' house."

She pulled it out and put it on. The package wraps rolled down the front porch steps, and suddenly, Samara felt a sense of unease creeping in.

"Hold on, that would mean someone had their eyes on me that night."

There was an eerie quietness in the air.

Samara quickly searched the pockets and discovered that the white rose from the café was still snuggled inside. The white rose had withered, but a mysterious sealed envelope was affixed. Samara quickly opened the envelope and lifted the paper to her eyes.

> You were so easy to find.
> I thought you might need your jacket.
> It would be a shame if you caught a cold or your death.

Samara's eyes darted around the neighborhood; she breathed heavily, panting with fear. Suddenly, her phone vibrated in her pocket. It was a text message from an unrecognizable number.

> "No matter where you go, no matter what you do, remember this: I'm always watching you!"

About the Author

Daniel Ortiz is a talented author who has quickly made a name for himself in suspense and thriller writing. He draws inspiration from his love of classic suspense novels and his fascination with the darker aspects of human nature. When not writing, Daniel enjoys exploring the outdoors, traveling, and spending time with his friends and family.

Scan the QR code below to find out more.

Linktr.ee/danielortz